EASTERN HEROES
ENTER THE DRAGON DISCUSSION WITH ALAN CANVAN
By Rick Baker

Alan Canvan edited Game of Death Redux. The edit only uses footage shot during the original production of The Game of Death and he recently completed a final version "Game of Death Redux 2.00" Alan is currently filming a new exciting Bruce Lee documentary to companion his new G.O.D Redux 2.00 edit.

RB - At the time of its release, Enter the Dragon was considered a groundbreaking film for several reasons. Firstly, it was one of the first movies to feature martial arts prominently, and it did so in a way that was both stylish and exciting. What initial impact did the movie have on you when you first saw it?

AC: My first viewing of Enter the Dragon was on videocassette in 1982. Although it played on a relatively small screen, its effect on me was monumental. In my opinion, it remains the standard by which all hand-to-hand action films are measured by. And as influential as it was on pop culture, it really towed the line between commercial and arthouse cinema in a way that's rarely seen today.

RB - **Enter the Dragon was one of the first movies to bring together international talent from both sides of the Pacific. The film was a co-production between Hong Kong's Golden Harvest studio and Warner Bros. Pictures, and it featured a diverse cast of actors from the US, Hong Kong, and other countries. How do you think this cross-cultural collaboration helped to broaden the appeal of the film and cemented its place in cinematic history?**

AC: Enter the Dragon's roots go back to a screenplay that Fred Weintraub developed in the late 1960's called Kelsey. The story followed three men of different ethnic backgrounds who band together to fight a common villain. The concept was ahead of its time both socially and in its aim to reach a wide demographic. Of course, when Warner Bros. got a glimpse of the film dailies, there was little doubt as to who the star of Enter the Dragon would be.

RB - Enter the Dragon was notable for its themes of honour, respect, and discipline. These themes were central to Bruce Lee's personal philosophy and were reflected in the movie's plot and characters. Did you find the films message of self-improvement and self-mastery resonated with audiences around the world, inspiring countless individuals to take up martial arts and to strive for personal excellence in their own lives?

AC: Enter the Dragon granted Bruce the opportunity to give the world its first genuine martial arts lesson on screen. And in doing so, he captivated audiences all over the globe. The influx of young men who signed up for martial art classes in the weeks and months following the film's release was something akin to a movement, so, in that respect, Bruce became an emissary and figurehead for positive change in people's lives. And that plays a huge role in why he's revered as the linchpin of everything martial today.

RB - Robert Clouse was chosen as the director of Enter the Dragon after Bruce Lee watched the fight scene he shot between Rod Taylor and William Smith in Darker than Amber. What do you think inspired Bruce about this scene (that was more of a violent brawl) as there were many other Directors that could have fit the bill E.g.) Richard Donner, Sam Peckinpah, or Sidney Lumet.

AC: I think the main appeal for Bruce was that Clouse filmed the close quarter combat in a cinema verité style that gave audiences the visceral sense of a primal ambush attack. Bruce was experimenting with elements of this in Game of Death, so I think that contributed to his interest in Clouse as a director. Of course, it helped that

Bob was a less expensive hire than the more popular directors you mentioned.

RB -At the end of the movie we see Bruce, with the scars across his face and torso, peer from behind a wall to give the thumbs up to Roper. Why do you think that image is so iconic?

AC: A big part of the reason why the depiction of Bruce with lacerations on his torso and cheeks resonates with audiences is because, visually, it correlates with war paint that ancient tribal warriors applied to their faces and bodies before going into battle. The image is iconic because it subliminally reinforces Bruce Lee as the pre-eminent warrior.

RB -You recently mentioned symbolism in many of the scenes in Enter the Dragon, one of them relates to the fight scene with Bob Wall. Can you expand on that for me?

AC: What's evident in the contest between Bruce and Bob Wall is the way in which Lee punishes O'Harra throughout the fight. His annihilation of O'Harra is not just physical, but emotional, as he effortlessly humiliates him in front of his men. The sequence culminates with O'Harra breaking a glass bottle and attempting to use the jagged edges to stab Lee, which symbolically acts as an inverse representation of Su Lin using the broken glass windowpane to commit suicide.

RB -After the opening fight with Sammo Hung at the monastery, comes a longer scene in the extended version that has Bruce speaking with the Shaolin Priest. Although Bruce's philosophy is interesting do you think this was better left in or removed? Which version of Enter the Dragon do you prefer?

ENTER THE DRAGON

THE IMMORTAL LEGACY OF BRUCE LEE'S ICONIC MARTIAL ARTS EPIC

As we celebrate the 50th anniversary of Enter the Dragon, it is worth taking a closer look at the film's lasting impact on both the action genre and Asian representation in Western media.

One of the most significant contributions of Enter the Dragon was its portrayal of martial arts as a serious and sophisticated discipline. Bruce Lee's character, Lee, is a martial arts master who emphasizes discipline and philosophy over brute force. This portrayal of martial arts not only elevated its status in popular culture but also helped to increase interest in the practice itself, leading to a surge in martial arts schools and practitioners.

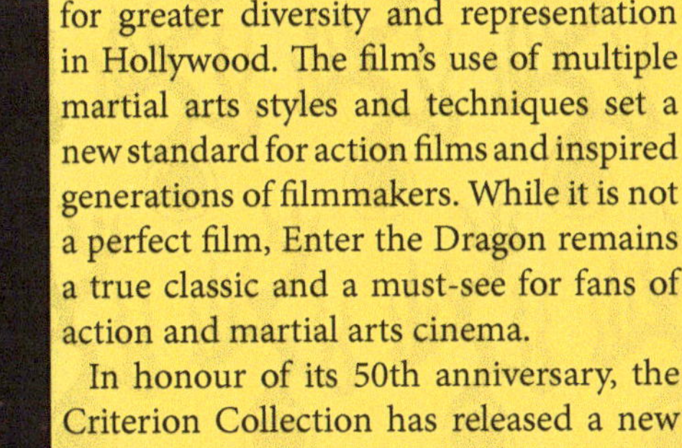

But Enter the Dragon's impact extended beyond the martial arts community. The film challenged Hollywood's lack of diversity by casting an Asian lead actor in a role that was not simply a stereotypical sidekick or villain. Bruce Lee's portrayal of Lee showcased his incredible martial arts skills and his charismatic personality, earning him a legion of fans around the world. The film's success paved the way for other Asian actors to take on leading roles in Hollywood, although progress in this area has been slow and there is still a long way to go.

Enter the Dragon also had a significant impact on the action genre, particularly in terms of its use of multiple martial arts styles and techniques. The film showcased different martial arts styles such as karate, judo, and kung fu, as well as Lee's unique style of Jeet Kune Do. This variety made the action scenes more dynamic and engaging, and inspired many filmmakers to explore different martial arts styles in their own films.

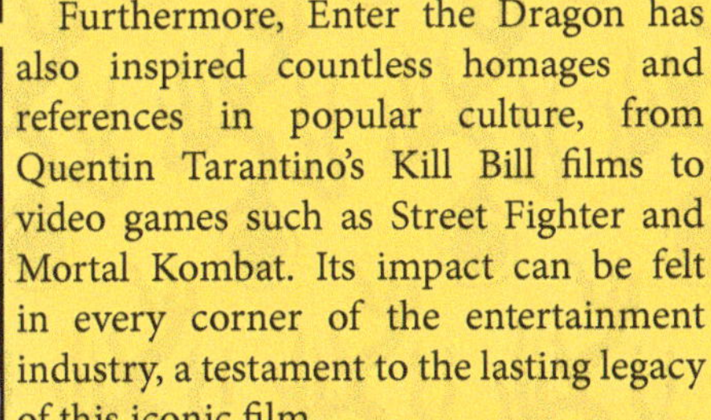

Despite its status as a classic film, Enter the Dragon is not without its flaws. Some critics have noted that the film perpetuates certain stereotypes, such as the portrayal of the villainous Mr Han as a stereotypical Asian despot. Others have criticized the lack of depth in some of the supporting characters and the somewhat simplistic plot. However, these criticisms do not detract from the film's overall impact and enduring popularity.

Enter the Dragon remains a landmark film that continues to inspire and entertain audiences 50 years after its release. Its pioneering casting of an Asian lead actor and its portrayal of martial arts as a sophisticated discipline paved the way for greater diversity and representation in Hollywood. The film's use of multiple martial arts styles and techniques set a new standard for action films and inspired generations of filmmakers. While it is not a perfect film, Enter the Dragon remains a true classic and a must-see for fans of action and martial arts cinema.

In honour of its 50th anniversary, the Criterion Collection has released a new Blu-ray edition of Enter the Dragon, featuring a restored 4K digital transfer and a host of special features. This release is a must-have for fans of the film and a great opportunity for new audiences to experience this timeless classic.

Furthermore, Enter the Dragon has also inspired countless homages and references in popular culture, from Quentin Tarantino's Kill Bill films to video games such as Street Fighter and Mortal Kombat. Its impact can be felt in every corner of the entertainment industry, a testament to the lasting legacy of this iconic film.

In conclusion, Enter the Dragon is a film that has transcended its genre and become a cultural touchstone. Its impact on Asian representation in Hollywood, martial arts culture, and the action genre cannot be overstated. As we look back on 50 years of this classic film, we can appreciate the lasting impact it has had on the world of cinema and beyond.

"To examine this movie further, I invited three friends who are respected in their fields and all share a passion for Bruce Lee: **Alan Canvan**, a filmmaker and director of Game of Death Redux 2.0; **Matthew Polly**, an American writer and best-selling author of Bruce Lee: A Life; **Frank Djeng**, a master of audio commentaries. I posed questions that would allow us to take a deeper dive into this iconic movie. Read on for their responses.

THE ENDURING INFLUENCE OF *BRUCE LEE*
A PERSONAL JOURNEY
By Rick Baker

*"IN THE BEGINNING THE WORLD FLIRTED WITH MARTIAL MOVIES –
BUT IT WAS NOT UNTILL BRUCE LEE CAME ALONG THAT WE FELL IN LOVE WITH THEM"*

In 1974, I sat in a movie theatre transfixed by a figure larger than life, radiating an aura of indefatigable energy, power, and sheer magnetic charisma. That figure was Bruce Lee. As I sat in awe of his performance in the "Enter the Dragon," it became evident that my life would never be the same again. His immense influence transformed me from an impressionable young guy into a lifelong devotee of martial arts and a chronicler of eastern cinema.

Bruce Lee was more than just an actor or a martial artist; he was a cultural phenomenon. His speed, agility, and strength, combined with his distinctive mix of charisma and coolness, captivated audiences around the world. However, the influence of Lee was not confined to his martial arts prowess. He was a philosopher who embodied his beliefs in every kick and punch he delivered. His aphorism, "Be water, my friend," became a guiding philosophy for me, a mantra that led me to embrace adaptability, fluidity, and resilience.

In my teens, inspired by Lee, I began practicing Karate, emulating his physical discipline and mental focus. Martial arts were more than a hobby or a way to keep fit—it was a way to connect with my idol, to walk, even if in a small way, the path that he had blazed. It was a discipline that taught me not only self-defence but also self-reliance, discipline, and respect, values that Bruce Lee himself exemplified.

By the late '80s, my passion for martial arts and Bruce Lee had taken a more public form. I started a magazine called "Eastern Heroes," dedicated to discussing and celebrating Bruce Lee and other martial art heroes from Hong Kong cinema. This publication provided an outlet to share my passion and connect with other like-minded enthusiasts. It was an avenue through which I could keep the spirit of Lee alive, discussing his philosophies, analysing his movies, and exploring his enduring impact.

As the years rolled by, my admiration for Lee never waned. I started another magazine specifically dedicated to Bruce Lee, keeping the torch of his legacy burning brightly. This magazine features special issues that delve deep into various facets of Lee's life, philosophies, and techniques, offering fans new insights into this enigmatic figure who continues to inspire millions.

Bruce Lee's influence extends far beyond individual fandoms. He ignited a global Kung Fu movie craze, opening the doors for a generation of martial artists and inspiring numerous martial art films. In Hollywood, a traditionally Western-dominated industry, Lee was a pioneering figure, challenging stereotypes and showcasing the artistry and depth of Eastern martial arts and philosophy.

Bruce Lee's untimely demise in 1973 sent shockwaves around the world. As we approach the 50th anniversary of his passing, it's astounding to see his popularity remains as potent as ever. His philosophies continue to inspire, his movies are still watched and studied, and his martial arts techniques are practiced by countless followers.

For many, Bruce Lee was a symbol of resilience, a beacon of perseverance, and a model of integrity. For me, his influence was transformative—it shaped my interests, career, and life philosophy. Lee once said, "The key to immortality is first living a life worth remembering." As we commemorate his life and legacy, it is evident that Bruce Lee, in his short yet impactful life, achieved immortality. His influence continues to resonate, inspiring new generations to embrace martial arts, to break barriers, and above all, to be like water, adapting, flowing, and overcoming obstacles in their paths.

AC: In my opinion, the theatrical version is superior. While I understand the intent of the scene with the Abott, it doesn't quite achieve what it sets out to do. The information on Han's backstory feels too expository and halts the pacing of the film, while the philosophical commentary on combat pales in comparison with the lesson Lee teaches his student in the following scene. It's also notable that, unlike other films that attempted to do the same thing, the philosophy presented in Enter the Dragon mostly avoids fortune cookie cliches, which truly elevates the material beyond what was typical in action cinema then or now.

RB - You, like me, really think highly about the soundtrack for Game of Death by John Barry. What are your thoughts on Lalo Schifrin's soundtrack? Brett Ratner loved it so much that he brought Lalo out of retirement to do the soundtrack for Rush Hour?

AC: Lalo Schifrin created a unique blend of jazz, funk and classical sounds that truly captured the spirit of the film. As with John Barry's score for Game of Death, Schifrin's score excels when it narrates the action in the film, but equally, when it uses the smaller moments to set up the bigger overtures. One of my favorite moments comes at the end of the film when the eerie carnival music plays over the image of Han's dead body impaled on the revolving door as Lee exits the mirror room. The somber notes that accompany Lee and Roper's thumbs up acknowledgment in the courtyard as the helicopters appear and the main theme kicks in is perfect. I'll also say that Schifrin's sampling of Bruce's war cry in the opening credit's theme was pure genius and one of the coolest moments in the history of cinema.

RB -In hindsight do you think do you think Enter the Dragon was Bruce Lee's defining role in terms of cementing his iconic status

to the world, or did he have better roles in his other films and the only reason Enter the Dragon is the most cited is due to it being a Hollywood production?

AC: It was certainly his defining role as a screen personality – less so as an actor. The character Bruce plays in Enter the Dragon is, in many ways, the classic 1970's film hero. Though his initial motive for accepting the mission is personal, by the end of the movie he's fighting for all mankind against the forces of oppression. In effect, when he defeats Han (and his army), he symbolically becomes the savior of the world. As far as cinematic archetypes go, it doesn't get any better than that. While the role doesn't allow him to express a full range of emotions in the way The Big Boss or The Orphan does, I believe it was the perfect vehicle to make Bruce Lee an international star.

RB -How did director Robert Clouse, manage to balance the themes of martial arts and espionage in Enter the Dragon?

AC: Robert Clouse doesn't get nearly enough credit for the success of Enter the Dragon. It's not an over generalization to say that he pioneered a soecufic cinematic staple which found its way into many of the hybrid action films that followed. In the wake of the film's box-office triumph, Marvel Comics created the Lee inspired character, Shang Chi, whose exploits in the Master of Kung Fu magazine drew heavily from the look and tone of Enter the Dragon. The series focused on a young Chinese Kung Fu prodigy who is recruited by British Intelligence to stop his evil warlord Father's attempts to dominate the world. It was brilliantly written by Doug Moench, who took the Kung Fu/Spy Thriller genre to new heights while simultaneously exploring many of the philosophical themes that Bruce had planned for his future movies. It also had

a huge influence on the father/son relationship between Luke and Anakin in George Lucas's Star Wars saga. To me, it's really a case of six degrees, as it's always been a strong hunch on my part that Lucas was equally inspired by Bruce Lee as he was by Akira Kurosawa.

RB -What was the significance of Bruce Lee's role as a writer and choreographer in the film, and how did it influence the final product?

AC: During filming, Bruce's primary concern was that Warner Bros. would cut down his screen time to favor John Saxon's character in post-production. To that end, he dug deep and gave them a physical performance that they couldn't deny. Obviously, the execution of his fight choreography was instrumental to how he was received by Western audiences. Beyond that though, Bruce made several contributions to the final cut of Enter the Dragon that changed the film for the better, including filming roughly 50% of the battle

in the hall of mirrors (following Clouse's departure for the US), writing dialogue for the Shaolin temple sequences and directing the fight with Sammo Hung that opens the movie. In the end, the final product was a true amalgam of both Bruce Lee and Robert Clouse's respective visions.

RB - Bruce also fought for the title of the film to be changed to "Enter the Dragon" when it was originally going to be called "Blood and Steel"?

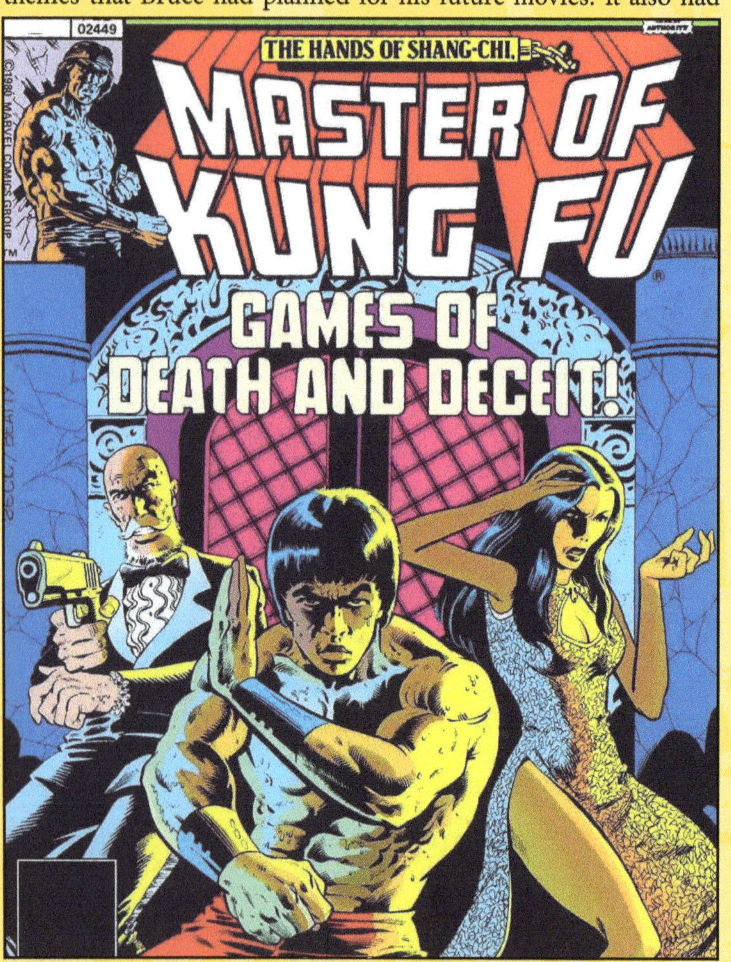

AC: Yes, that was a point of contention between Bruce and the studio throughout filming. They wanted to change the title from "Blood and Steel" to "Han's Island." Bruce had held back the title "Enter the Dragon" for his directorial debut (eventually named Way of the Dragon) and wanted it be used as his introduction to the international market.

RB -How did Bruce Lee's own martial arts philosophy and technique come across in his portrayal of the character of Lee in the film?

AC: The philosophy presented in Enter the Dragon barely scratched the surface of Bruce's approach to the martial arts, but it did expose audiences to a few basic principles that shaped his outlook on combat. In terms of techniques, there's a tendency to confuse what Bruce did in the movie with what he would've applied in the real world. The opening match between Bruce and Sammo is a prime example of how the line is blurred between JKD and Screen JKD. Fans often cite the duel as proof of Lee being a good candidate for the UFC, forgetting that he had no interest in participating in any kind of sport combat – including mixed martial arts. Why? Because no matter how fluid and alive the sport is, there are still rules - and those rules would've hindered Bruce's most effective fighting tactics. And though that scene had a profound effect on the sport of MMA, it's important to remember that it was done to service the character in the film, and not indicative of a new sport that Lee was trying to create. Father of MMA? Not quite, although I understand why he's been referred to as that.

RB -What was the impact of Enter the Dragon on the careers of the supporting actors, such as John Saxon and Jim Kelly?

AC: John Saxon used to joke about having a dream where he was getting robbed and the offender, upon recognizing Saxon, stops and asks, "What was it like working with Bruce Lee?" (Laughs). Career-wise, Enter the Dragon certainly raised John Saxon and Jim Kelly's profiles within the industry, but, more importantly, it gave them a cult status within the martial arts community. I think part of the reason why their characters are so memorable is because they were

allies to the most famous and influential martial arts actor who ever lived.

RB -In what ways did the film subvert traditional Hollywood stereotypes of Asian characters and actors?

AC: Well, it dispelled the notion that all Asian men were weaklings, but, on the flipside, it gave birth to the stereotype that all young Chinese males were Kung Fu masters in disguise. (Laughter.) That became somewhat of a limiting model for Asian actors in the last 50 years.
RB -We've discussed Bruce Lee's sexuality in previous chats. Do you think that Clouse sexualized Bruce Lee in Enter the Dragon?

AC: I don't think Clouse sexualized him per se - Bruce 's sex appeal naturally came through in all his performances - but Clouse delivered a portrait that spotlighted Lee's inherent sensuality on screen. It's fair to say that one of the things that Enter the Dragon did, was take the traditional image of the Kung Fu Sage and make it sexy for modern audiences.

RB -What can the film's portrayal of masculinity and gender dynamics teach us about the cultural values of the 1970s?

AC: What's interesting is how Enter the Dragon divides the James Bond archetype into two characters: Lee is the ambassador of justice with the near superhuman physical skills working with British Intelligence, while Roper is the stylish playboy who lives on borrowed time and romances the ladies. The Williams character falls

somewhere in between the two, but mostly reflects the "supercool stud" persona found in blaxploitation films from that era. One thing I find interesting is the fact that even though Lee and Williams never converse, there's a peripheral awareness and respect that exists between them.
RB -In what ways did Bruce Lee's own life and experiences inform the character of Lee in Enter the Dragon?

AC: It was a role that he had been prepping for most of his adult life. He began shaping it in the early 1960s when he started to teach self-defense and continued to hone it while he tutored celebrities in Hollywood. Matthew Polly hit the nail on the head when he said that each private lesson Bruce gave in Tinseltown was essentially a paid audition.

RB - In the absence of Bruce Lee's casting, do you believe that Enter the Dragon would have encountered significant challenges in generating an impact or even progressing into production? Alternatively, do you opine that the triumph of the 1972 television series "Kung Fu," which portrayed the exploits of Kwai Chang Caine, a Shaolin monk journeying across the American Old West, would have sufficed to garner approval for the project without necessitating the inclusion of an Asian protagonist?

AC: Based on the success of the Kung Fu TV Series, I'm certain that a Hollywood produced martial arts movie was on the horizon. Would it have been as successful without Bruce Lee? Not a chance. While producers saw the potential in Asian action cinema, they really couldn't predict how influential the genre would be over the next five decades. That would never have happened without the presence of Bruce Lee.

RB -Given my personal experience as a former cocaine addict, I perceive Bruce Lee's cocaine usage to have likely been constrained. Upon examining the letters, he exchanged with Bob Baker, it appears that his consumption was more sporadic and dependent on the arrival of packages from Bob. Additionally, considering the challenges Bruce would have faced in accessing cocaine in Hong Kong, its usage would have been further restricted. Nevertheless, being in the United States while filming Enter the Dragon and at that time was very fashionable and would have potentially been easier access to the substance. In light of these circumstances, do you believe Bruce Lee exercised sufficient prudence to abstain

from cocaine during the filming period? And had he lived do you think he would have found his rock bottom like others stars did now having the money and easy access to facilitate his needs?
AC: I agree that, in the last year of his life, Bruce was less of a stone-cold junkie than a progressive binger. That said, Bruce was an extremist, and the probability of him developing a major drug issue following the success of Enter the Dragon seemed likely. Would

cocaine have killed him, or would he have eventually checked into rehab, overcome his addiction, and wrote a self-help book to promote on talk show circuits? It's difficult to say. It could have gone either way, really.

RB - Bruce Lee's character in Enter the Dragon was named "Lee." Do you think this was simply for the sake of simplicity, as Bruce himself was an Asian lead, or is there a deeper significance behind it? Furthermore, do you believe this naming choice

might have been suggested by Bruce during script discussions?

AC: The character's full name is Jun Keung Lee, which was deliberate choice on Bruce's part. The English translation of "Jun Keung" means to rise up strongly. So, while the surname was eponymous and immediately identified Bruce to Western audiences, there was a more to it than just simple convenience.

RB -In the movie, we notice that each of the three rooms on Han's island, designated for "Roper," "Williams," and "Lee," appeared to be tailored to their specific needs. What do you think was the significance behind this?

AC: It makes sense that Han would research potential recruits for his criminal empire. One of the more effective ways to lure people in, is to show appreciation for their interests. There's a wonderful, deleted scene that sees Lee enter his room and notice one of his books displayed on the table. Why did Han place the book there? Was he sending a message, or simply appealing to Lee's ego? Incidentally, the Chinese title of the front cover reads: SHAOLIN TEMPLE - JUN KEUNG KUNE PRACTICE VOLUME 3. Now there's a prop I'd love to see on Heritage Auctions.

RB -In Enter the Dragon, Bruce Lee exhibits a wide range of emotions throughout various scenes, as observed from a thorough analysis of numerous photos. This prompts the question of whether these expressive capabilities were honed during his early years as a child actor, or if they were primarily influenced by his martial arts training, thereby eliciting the multitude of facial expressions he displays on screen.

AC: Bruce's first love was performing. He grew up imitating cinema icons like Charlie Chaplin, Jerry Lewis and James Dean. He had an equal passion for playing nerdy characters as he did heroes. For instance, the Paul Wei Ping-ao role in Way of the Dragon was based on a campy gay character that Bruce would imitate for shits 'n' giggles. Look at the movies he starred in as a teenager or the telephone repairman character he invented for Fist of Fury. In many ways, Bruce was a character actor in a leading man's body.

RB - Lastly it is imperative to examine the profound impact that Enter the Dragon had upon you upon its initial viewing. Furthermore, I am interested in gathering your personal reflections on Bruce Lee, encompassing his prowess as an actor and martial artist, as well as the influential role he assumed in shaping your present-day life.

AC: Bruce Lee was my childhood idol. As a youth, I studied his life and films with near religious fervor, but, over the years, I've come to better understand who he was (and wasn't) as an artist and a man. One thing that's become transparent to me is just how reductive it is to view him solely through the lens of martial arts. Yes, the study of combat was a huge part of his life, but it was only one facet of his character, And, to be perfectly honest, the aspect that I find the least interesting in his body of work. He had similar passions, including film, acting, fight choreography, dancing, music, and art. And like many young artists he struggled with his perceptions of ego and identity.

To understand Bruce Lee, the paradigm shift needs to begin by dispelling certain myths: He was not a fighter, although he could fight. He was not a philosopher, though he could wax philosophical on subjects that held his interest. He was a Zen mystic and punk rock rebel. He was highly intelligent, and equally foolish. Tough as nails and quite fragile. If there's a takeaway in terms of an influence on me today, it's recognizing those qualities in myself, as well as in others. And in the cosmic scheme of things, that's pretty fuckin' cool.

Special thank you to Alan Canvan for taking part in this interview

Mathew Polly is a renowned American author and former martial artist with a deep passion for martial arts. Throughout his career, he has delved into the intricate world of combat and shared his knowledge and experiences through his captivating books. Some of his notable works include "American Shaolin," "Tapped Out," and "Bruce Lee: A Life."

Polly's journey began after graduating from Topeka West High School, and in 1992, he embarked on a life-changing adventure. At the age of 21, he made the bold decision to take a break from his studies at Princeton University and set off for China. His destination was the legendary Shaolin Temple, the very birthplace of Chan (Zen) Buddhism and kung fu.

During his time at the Shaolin Temple, Polly's training was intense and transformative. Although some critics questioned the efficacy of his experiences, he dedicated himself to the rigorous program designed to enthral foreigners. Polly resided at the temple for two years, becoming the first American ever accepted as a Shaolin disciple.

Under the guidance of the revered Shaolin monks, Polly honed his skills tirelessly. He devoted seven hours a day, six days a week, to various training disciplines, which included running, breathing exercises, calisthenics, Kung Fu, and gymnastics. Through sheer dedication and perseverance, he emerged as a formidable kick boxer, even triumphing in a challenge match against a kung fu master from another province.

One remarkable feat of Polly's training involved the development of his "iron forearm" technique. By subjecting his arm to relentless impact against a tree for 30 minutes each day, calluses formed, rendering his arm impervious to pain. This specialized expertise became a testament to his unwavering commitment to mastering the martial arts. Matthew Polly's captivating journey, shared through his books, offers readers a window into the rich world of martial arts and the profound personal growth that can be attained through dedication and perseverance. His works continue to inspire and educate martial arts enthusiasts around the globe, solidifying his reputation as a respected authority in the field.

RB - In the absence of Bruce Lee's casting, do you believe that "Enter the Dragon" would have encountered significant challenges in generating an impact or even progressing into production? Alternatively, do you opine that the triumph of the 1972 television series "Kung Fu," which portrayed the exploits of Kwai Chang Caine, a Shaolin monk journeying across the American Old West, would have sufficed to garner approval for the project without necessitating the inclusion of an Asian protagonist?

MP - Without Bruce Lee, Enter the Dragon never gets made. Bruce was personal friends with Fred Weintraub, the producer, and Ted Ashley, the president of Warner Bros. Weintraub was only able to convince Ashley to greenlight the movie because of that personal relationship with Bruce and because Bruce's previous three Golden Harvest movies had smashed East Asian box office records. Even with all that, Warner Bros. initially only invested $250,000, a miniscule amount. The budget for The Exorcist, which was made the same year, was $11 million. Without Bruce Lee, Hollywood would probably have eventually made a kung fu genre flick, but it wouldn't have been set in Hong

Kong and it would have starred a white actor like David Carradine.
RB - In the initial radio advertisements preceding the release of the film, Warner Bros. promoted John Saxon as "Roper," Jim Kelly as "Williams," and Bruce Lee as "Lee." During that time, Roper was the actor receiving the highest salery in the movie. However, after the movie premiered, the radio spots were modified to emphasize Bruce Lee as the leading figure by declaring him as "Black Belt Hall of Fame Bruce Lee as Lee." Considering these circumstances, it raises the question of whether Warner Bros. possessed foresight regarding the profound influence the film would exert on its audience, both domestically in the United States and on a global scale.

MP - Prior to Enter the Dragon, no Chinese male actor had ever starred in a Hollywood movie. If you read the script, it is obvious that John Saxon's character, Roper, is the better part with a complete arc from roguish mercenary to hero. It was quite reasonable for Warner Bros. to assume Saxon would be the better marketing angle for the movie. It was from sheer force of will and whatever X-factor makes someone a star that Bruce Lee dominates Enter the Dragon. As soon as the initial audiences saw it, it became obvious to Warner Bros as well who was the main draw.

RB - Pre-production of the film encountered certain challenges, primarily attributed to Bruce Lee's purported nervousness. However, there are indications of additional conflicts transpiring behind the scenes that significantly impeded the filming process. Consequently, it would be valuable to explore this aspect further. Furthermore, I would appreciate your insights regarding the potential implications of Bruce Lee's cocaine usage, as it seemingly contributed to his noticeable weight loss, which was prominently observable on screen.

MP - The recently released letters that Bruce Lee wrote to his student

the period he was filming Enter the Dragon was not only a result of stress, as was previously assumed, but also was likely exacerbated by cocaine usage.

RB - Given my personal experience as a former cocaine addict, I perceive Bruce Lee's cocaine usage to have likely been constrained. Upon examining the letters he exchanged with Bob Baker, it appears that his consumption was more sporadic and dependent on the arrival of packages from Bob. Additionally, considering the challenges Bruce would have faced in accessing cocaine in Hong Kong, its usage would have been further restricted. Nevertheless, being in the United States while filming "Enter the Dragon" and at that time was very fashionable and would have potentially been easier access to the substance. In light of these circumstances, do you believe Bruce Lee exercised sufficient prudence to abstain from cocaine during the filming period? And had he lived do you think he would have found his rock bottom like others stars did now having the money and easy access to facilitate his needs?

MP - It is impossible to know if he was or was not using during filming or whether he would or would not have developed a serious problem if he had lived. But given how disciplined and ambitious Bruce was as a martial artist and filmmaker, my guess is he would have stopped using it before spiralling out of control.

RB - To what extent do you perceive Bruce Lee's portrayal in "Enter the Dragon" as having been subjected to sexualisation? Given his remarkable physical appearance as an attractive Asian actor, it is plausible to consider the appeal he may have held for Western women. Moreover, do you believe this factor contributed to expanding his audience, despite the prevailing perception of him as a revered masculine figure and influential role model for men? It is worth contemplating whether women attending screenings during the film's initial release might have derived enjoyment from the movie not solely due to the combat sequences, but also from Bruce Lee's undeniable on-screen allure which reminds me of Elvis who was just acting natural on screen but his body language was very appealing to his female audience that went beyond his music.

MP - Bruce liked taking his shirt off on film. He liked doing it off screen as well. He was proud of his body and had put in a lot

Bob Baker in 1972-3 reveal that Bruce had developed a fondness for cocaine. It is not clear how often or how much he used, but it is important to remember that in the early 1970s cocaine was the hip new drug in Hollywood and most people in the industry didn't think it was that dangerous. Now we know better. At any rate, I think it is safe to assume that some of Bruce's more erratic behaviour during

MP - Anyone interested in the answer to this question can read my book, Bruce Lee: A Life.
Note from editor – available to buy from all good on line book stores.

RB - In the film "Enter the Dragon," Bruce Lee undertook the task of writing and directing the initial scene, despite it being the final sequence to be filmed. Considering this circumstance, to what extent do you believe Bruce Lee contributed to his character's portrayal on screen throughout the entire movie? Can we perceive a distinct presence that embodies more of Bruce Lee himself, rather than merely his character, "Lee"?

MP - The initial scene set at the "Shaolin Temple," were not about injecting Bruce himself into the movie but about controlling his public image of "Bruce Lee" as a defender of the Chinese people.

of work developing his ripped physique. I'm sure it was not lost on him or the director the effect a bare-chested Bruce Lee would have on some members of the audience, both female and male.

RB - In "Enter the Dragon," Bruce Lee exhibits a wide range of emotions throughout various scenes, as observed from a thorough analysis of numerous photos. This prompts the question of whether these expressive capabilities were honed during his early years as a child actor, or if they were primarily influenced by his martial arts training, thereby eliciting the multitude of facial expressions he displays on screen.

MP - Bruce Lee was an actor long before he was a martial artist. He came from an acting family. His father got him his first film roles. He was what we would now call a "nepo baby." He took acting very seriously and was always striving to get better at it. His expressiveness on screen was due to his background as an actor. If anyone needs proof, just watch the films of Chuck Norris, who was a martial artist first before he became an actor.

RB - Can you shed light on any specific scenes that were particularly challenging to film and required extensive planning and coordination?

He was not a Shaolin monk, nor had he ever trained at the Shaolin Temple. He was an actor who was also extremely good at martial arts. In his previous three films he had played a character who had defended Chinese immigrant laborers from evil Thai thugs (The Big Boss), Chinese students under Japanese occupation (Fist of Fury), Chinese restaurant workers being exploited by the Italian mafia (Way of the Dragon). The initial script cast Bruce as a James Bond figure working for the (hated colonial) British empire. By turning himself into a Shaolin monk who was avenging the murder of his sister, he was reaffirming his image as a protector of the Chinese people.

RB - In the context of Bruce Lee's involvement in the Hollywood movie "Enter the Dragon," it is pertinent to consider the individual or individuals upon whom he may have drawn inspiration for his portrayal. Given the necessity for him to exhibit charisma both in his acting and on-screen combat skills to showcase versatility, it is likely that he aimed to avoid being typecast solely as a Kung Fu star, thereby capitalizing on his newfound success. With this in mind, who do you believe Bruce Lee sought to emulate or shape his persona after for his role in "Enter the Dragon"?

MP - Bruce Lee told friends that his return to Hong Kong was a direct emulation of Clint Eastwood, who had gone to Italy to make several Spaghetti Westerns as proof that he could be a bankable Hollywood movie star. Hong Kong was Bruce's Italy, and his Golden Harvest movies were his Spaghetti Westerns. It is reasonable to

assume Bruce was thinking about Eastwood's "Man with No Name" persona while making Enter the Dragon.

RB - In the production of the film "Enter the Dragon," it is of interest to explore the specific methodology employed to bring the project to fruition, particularly regarding the selection of the cast members. With the exception of notable individuals such as "John Saxon" and "Ahna Capri," the majority of the cast consisted of relatively unfamiliar faces to Western audiences. Consequently, what are your thoughts on the modality utilized to secure the necessary resources for the creation of "Enter the Dragon," as well as the casting process undertaken, considering the relatively unknown status of the majority of the cast members in relation to Western viewership?

MP - Enter the Dragon was an experiment, which very few people at the time believed would work. As a result, Warner Bros only invested a tiny amount of money, leaving the producers with little choice but to hire whoever was cheapest for almost every role including the writer, director, and most of the cast. It was basically an independent movie.

RB - Considering Bruce Lee's hypothetical survival, it raises speculation regarding his future trajectory within the film industry. Would he have proceeded with the production of a sequel to his renowned work, "Enter the Dragon," while persisting in his dedication to martial arts-based films during the interim? Furthermore, do you believe he would have revisited the unfinished project, "Game of Death"? In light of his improved financial standing, he would have possessed the means to halt the original filming and potentially re-shoot it with a substantially augmented budget, capitalizing on his accumulated directing experience from collaborating with Robert Clouse. With his elevated prominence and enhanced reputation, the world would

have presented boundless opportunities for him to explore.

MP - He was in talks with Warner Bros. to make two sequels to "Enter the Dragon". That is why Ted Ashley bent to Bruce's demand to change the name of the movie from "Han's Island" to "Enter the Dragon," which no one at Warner Bros liked. The success of Enter the Dragon would have given Bruce all sorts of opportunities to make other films. How long that opportunity lasted would have depended on the box office results of his next films. But I'm sure he would have attempted to complete Game of Death. He had been trying to tell the same story (the mystical martial arts quest movie) since The Silent Flute. It was near and dear to his heart.

RB - Lastly, it is imperative to examine the profound impact that "Enter the Dragon" had upon you upon its initial viewing. Furthermore, I am interested in gathering your personal reflections on Bruce Lee, encompassing his prowess as an actor and martial artist, as well as the influential role he assumed in shaping your present-day life.

MP - Unlike the other icons of the 20th century (Elvis Presley, Marilyn Monroe, James Dean), Bruce was more of a missionary than he was a celebrity. His religion was the martial arts, and he sought to spread their influence through the popular medium of film. With Enter the Dragon, he succeeded beyond his wildest dreams (and his dreams were pretty wild). As producer Fred Weintraub put it, "Every town in American had a church and a beauty parlour. After Enter the Dragon, there was a church, a beauty parlour, and a karate studio with a picture of Bruce Lee." I was one of the tens of millions who took up the study of the martial arts after watching Enter the Dragon, and it changed my life for the better.

Special Thank you Matthew for taking part in this Q&A.

Interview with FRANK DJENG

A Hong Kong native who's known affectionately by Hong Kong Cinema fans worldwide as the "Master of Remaster", Frank Djeng was instrumental in bringing hundreds of classic Hong Kong action titles to North America in their original aspect ratio and with improved English subtitles when he was Marketing Manager for Tai Seng Entertainment from 1996 to 2008. He's also the long time co-host of the Kung Fu Superhero Extravaganza Panel at the famous San Diego Comic Con since 1998, and he will be co-hosting there for the 26th time in 2023. He's now widely considered to be one of the best audio commentators for Hong Kong cinema releases on Blu-Ray and 4K UHD, recording close to 50 commentaries a year for such prestige boutique labels as Arrow, Criterion, Eureka, 88 Films, Shout! Factory and Radiance Films.

What impact did Bruce Lee's "Enter the Dragon" have on you when you first saw it? Do you believe that today's audiences, who have been exposed to martial arts movies, will have a similar experience? Or was the kung fu movie craze of the 70s a unique phenomenon in the Western world during that era?

FRANK: I came to "Enter the Dragon" rather late actually--I first saw it on laserdisc in the early 90's and I remembered being very impressed by the fight scenes, particularly the scene at the dungeon, and Lee's agility and speed of his attacks. I also found the final fight with Shek Kin to be rather disappointing and anticlimactic--I've always felt that Lee should've fought Bolo in the end instead. Before "Enter the Dragon", the only other Bruce Lee film I've seen was "Fist of Fury" as a kid when I saw it at the Golden Harvest Cinema in Hong Kong in 1980 when it was re-released to include the controversial "Chinese and Dogs not allowed" scene which was cut from the initial theatrical release. I found Lee to be more impressive

in "Fist of Fury" overall, simply because of how much he dominated the film from beginning to end.

I believe today's audiences will still be mesmerized by Bruce Lee if they watch this film today, even after being exposed to films by Jackie Chan, Jet Li, Donnie Yen, etc. Lee's swiftness, body movements, and his charisma were second to none and you simply

can't take your eyes off the screen whenever he's on it.   Although I also agree that the kung fu movie craze of the 70's was a rather unique phenomenon in the Western world that coincides with the

social environment at that time and how minorities, especially African Americans and Asian overseas, could relate to Bruce Lee as someone who was fighting against the system for social justice and inequalities that they encounter in their daily lives. They saw how Bruce was able to beat the system with his sheer strength of will and incredible martial arts skills. And as a result these folks, and I don't mean just the minorities but also those who felt suppressed, or bullied at their everyday lives, thought, "If Bruce can do it, then I can do it too!" which of course led to so many Westerners learning martial arts, not just for self-defense but also to elevate their own self-esteem and confidence. So the 70's was a perfect moment in time of history for kung fu movies to thrive and flourish.

RICK: Enter the Dragon was one of the first movies to bring together international talent from both sides of the Pacific. The film was a co-production between Hong Kong's Golden Harvest studio and Warner Bros. Pictures, and it featured a diverse cast of actors from the US, Hong Kong, and other countries. How do you think this cross-cultural collaboration helped to broaden the appeal of the film and cemented its place in cinematic history?

FRANK: I look at this film as an extension of what Bruce had already done in his previous film "Way of the Dragon" where he fought a non-Chinese fighter (Chuck Norris)—In "Enter the Dragon" he would have non-Chinese fighters like Jim Kelly and John Saxton sharing precious screen time with him. And the idea of having an Asian lead fighting non-Asian opponents would certainly extend to Hong Kong films in the 80's with Jackie Chan (Wheels On Meals, Armour of God), Donnie Yen (In The Line of Duty and Tiger Cage

films) and even with the films starring Cynthia Rothrock but with the gender and race reversed by having a Non-Asian lead fighting Asian opponents.

I also look at this film as a textbook example of how to properly introduce someone who's a virtual unknown outside of Asia to the rest of the world and makes you wonder how Golden Harvest could've been so wrong when they tried to do the same with Jackie Chan with "Battle Creek Brawl" with disastrous results.

But make no mistake— "Enter the Dragon" was iconic in martial arts film history with its introduction of Bruce Lee to the rest of the world on the cusp of his global fame, and because Lee has already

passed away by the time the film was released, it also added a mythical quality to his legacy which I think is why we're still talking about him and his films 50 years after his passing.

RICK: In what ways did the film subvert traditional Hollywood stereotypes of Asian characters and actors?

FRANK: Sadly, the film didn't subvert traditional Hollywood stereotypes of Asian characters and actors enough for me. While it's great to see Bruce Lee and Shek Kin as both the leading man and the leading villain respectively in a major Hollywood production, and presenting Asian men as strong and powerful instead of the weak stereotypes that we usually see in Hollywood films (More on that later), ENTER THE DRAGON was still hampered by several factors that prevented it from being the Hollywood film that should've given Asians major representation. First, Bruce's screen time was compromised by the time spent on other characters like the ones played by Jim Kelly and John Saxon. Second, Bruce's love interest in the film, Mei Ling (Played by Betty Chung), hardly had any characterization that's on par with Nora

Miao in her previous two films with Lee and was treated more as a decorative "vase" kind of role. Similarly, one can also say that Bolo Yeung's character was severely undermined—the film presented him as this formidable fighter from the moment you saw him waiting for the landing parties by the pier, and you had all this build up and anticipation of him eventually going into action, but he didn't even get to fight Bruce in the end!

Then there's the (retroactively speaking) ugly stereotyping of the "oriental" elements in the film that just don't sit comfortably with a native Chinese viewer like myself and which probably was responsible for the film's relatively low box office in Hong Kong compared to Lee's other films. You have women of all races wearing "Cheongsan" dresses, you have *Japanese* Sumo wrestlers in the banquet sequence (why?), and you have all the henchmen wearing karate robes when they should really be wearing Chinese-style clothing like the kind that Donnie Yen wears in his "Ip Man" films. It's almost as if Robert Clouse simply wanted to include anything that looks "Oriental" regardless

of their origin in the film to satisfy Westerner's preconception of how Orientals should look, similar to how a Chinese restaurant in the USA must serve Sweet and Sour Pork and General Tsao's Chicken even though both dishes are not found in most Chinese restaurants in Hong Kong, therefore these "Hollywood" stereotypes certainly weren't very "politically correct" and were downright offensive when viewed through the contemporary eyes. So while it's pretty gratifying to see Asians represented in a much more positive way than before in "Enter the Dragon", there were still elements in the film that showed that Hollywood just loves to display the "exoticism" of Asian culture, and they still do to this day.

RICK: Do you think "Enter the Dragon" would have faced significant challenges, in making an impact or even getting made if Bruce Lee had not been cast in it? Alternatively, do you believe that the success of the 1972 television series "Kung Fu," which depicted the adventures of Kwai Chang Caine, a Shaolin monk traveling through the American Old West, would have been enough to gain approval for the project without requiring an Asian protagonist?

FRANK: It would have been quite a challenge to have made "Enter the Dragon" without Bruce and even if it was made without out, it wouldn't have the same worldwide impact. I can't think of anyone who could've replaced Bruce, let alone equalled him, in "Enter the Dragon". The closest person I could think of would be Jimmy Wang Yu but Yu didn't have the same kind of charisma as Bruce, and his fighting style was not as elegant and unique.

"Kung Fu" might be enough to move "Enter the Dragon" forward without an Asian protagonist, but the film wouldn't have the same level of success, because whoever that would've replaced Bruce Lee was no Bruce Lee. With all due respect to the late David Carradine, even if he was cast as the lead for "Enter the Dragon", it just wouldn't have the same impact.

RICK: To what extent do you perceive Bruce Lee's portrayal in "Enter the Dragon" as having been subjected to sexualisation? Given his remarkable physical appearance as an attractive Asian actor, it is plausible to consider the appeal he may have held for Western women. Moreover, do you believe this factor

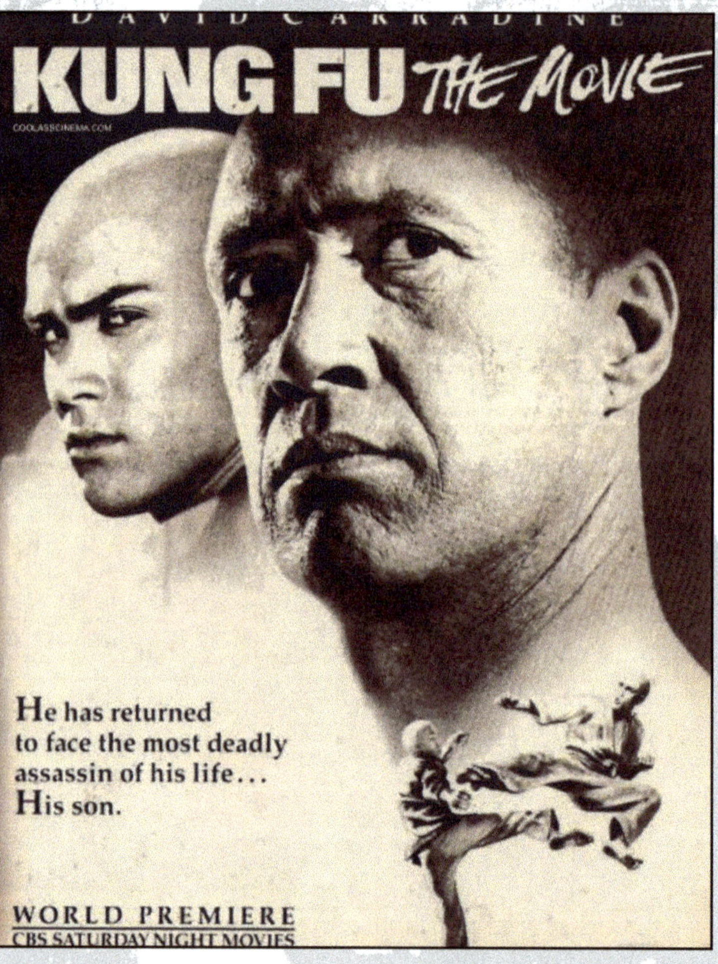

contributed to expanding his audience, despite the prevailing perception of him as a revered masculine figure and influential role model for men? It is worth contemplating whether women attending screenings during the film's initial release might have derived enjoyment from the movie not solely due to the combat sequences, but also from Bruce Lee's undeniable on-screen allure which reminds me of Elvis who was just acting natural on screen but his body language was very appealing to his female audience that went beyond his music.

FRANK: Interesting question. I am not sure if Western women were really the target audience for "Enter the Dragon" to be honest but surely some Westerners, both male and female, would be shocked by seeing such a strong, masculine Asian men on screen, which is not something that Asian men in the US were thought of because in Hollywood movies at the time, there were generally very few kind of strong roles for Asian men. You either play a Japanese soldier that eventually get killed at the end, or you could play a houseboy like Cato in the Peter Sellers

Inspector Clouseau/Pink Panther films. And even before "Enter the Dragon" Bruce Lee was already the exception by exhibiting a strong persona during his GREEN HORNET days. Asian women had somewhat more interesting parts in Hollywood films, but they were usually either geisha girls, prostitutes, or girlfriends of white leading men like William Holden in LOVE IS A MANY SPLENDORED THINGS.

Most Asian audiences in Hong Kong idolized Westerners--

your typical white knight. And as a result, "Enter the Dragon" and other Bruce Lee films made Westerners begin to think of Asian men as also capable of being strong and heroic.

While I can't say for sure how much of his on-screen allure appealed to the non-Asian female audiences, I think Bruce Lee just hit a certain moment in history where people in all parts of the world were looking for that kind of hero.

they thought everything from the West was better, which is why Hollywood films were so popular in Hong Kong (and still are). Then Bruce Lee came along and it was disruptive to the film industry both in Hong Kong and overseas—In Hong Kong, his onscreen allure generated a lot of pride amongst the local Chinese moviegoers who finally have someone of their own to cheer, admire and idolize (never mind the fact that Bruce was born in San Francisco and not Hong Kong!). In the West, huge numbers of both whites and minorities, particularly African Americans, love Kung Fu movies. They were able to identify Bruce Lee's characters in his films not just because he also stood for social justice, but for the simple reason that he's not

RICK: In "Enter the Dragon," Bruce Lee exhibits a wide range of emotions throughout various scenes, as observed from a thorough analysis of numerous photos. This prompts the question of whether these expressive capabilities were honed during his early years as a child actor, or if they were primarily influenced by his martial arts training, thereby eliciting the multitude of facial expressions he displays on screen.

FRANK: I feel it's a combination of both—Lee's experience as both a child and teen actor in films such as THE KID, THE ORPHANS and THE THUNDERSTORM certainly gave him plenty of opportunities

to honed his crafts—Remember, he acted in 26 films prior to "The Big Boss"! Lee's martial training with the expressiveness of his facial gestures certainly enhanced the intensity of his emotions not only in "Enter the Dragon" but also in his other Golden Harvest films, particularly in the fight scenes.

RICK: Considering Bruce Lee's hypothetical survival, it raises speculation regarding his future trajectory within the film industry. Would he have proceeded with the production of a sequel to his renowned work, "Enter the Dragon," while persisting in his dedication to martial arts-based films during the interim? Furthermore, do you believe he would have revisited the unfinished project, "Game of Death"? In light of his improved financial standing, he would have possessed the means to halt the original filming and potentially re-shoot it with a substantially augmented budget, capitalizing on his accumulated directing experience from collaborating with Robert Clouse. With his elevated prominence and enhanced reputation, the world would have presented boundless opportunities for him to explore.

FRANK: Well we can only speculate can't we? One thing that has always fascinated me was the final fight scene in "Game of Death" when Lee fought Karem Abdul-Jabbar who was Lee's student, and in that fight scene Karem was also using Jeet Kune Do moves on Lee. It's as if Lee was facing his own demon—he's fighting another version of himself who's taller, bigger and stronger, so how could he top that fight after he's already fought himself? I don't know whether Lee would've reshot "Game" but he would certainly have finished it

by completing the rest of the scenes. "Enter the Dragon 2" would probably have happened as well unless Bruce disliked the idea of having sequels to his films.

To me the more interesting question that we will never know the answer of would be whether Jackie Chan would become as popular as he was if Bruce Lee is still alive, and whether the kung fu comedy genre pioneered by Chan would have existed.

RICK: In the film "Enter the Dragon," Bruce Lee undertook the task of writing and directing the opening initial scene, despite it being the final sequence to be filmed. Considering this circumstance, to what extent do you believe Bruce Lee contributed to his character's portrayal on screen throughout the entire movie? Can we perceive a distinct presence that embodies more of Bruce Lee himself rather than merely his character, "Lee"?

FRANK: I honestly doubt Bruce Lee was able to contribute much to his character's portrayal on screen for the majority of the film with the screenplay being not written by him, but by Michael Allin. And I don't know how involved Bruce was in the screenwriting process (whether Allin sought Lee's inputs or took some of Lee's ideas and incorporated them into his screenplay for instance). There's a rather generic feel to Lee's character once he sets off for Han's Island, with all the philosophical musings we saw in the opening of the film out of the window, so to speak. It's almost as if there were two characters played by Bruce Lee—The one before he went to the island and the one after—and that Allin wasn't sure what kind of lines Lee should

be saying once he's joined by the others so for the majority part of the film, with the exception of lines such as "Boards don't hit back", I certainly sensed a "cardboard" feel to Lee's character as he just went through the motions of being a spy and spewing sappy dialogue to Mei Ling. For the scenes that Lee himself wrote such as the opening scenes with Roy Chiao, you could definitely feel that's Bruce Lee being Bruce Lee and not the Lee character in the film, which makes his character much more multi-dimensional.

As much as the film was celebrated for combining martial arts action with James Bond-like elements as well as with Blaxploitation which at that time was getting popular, these elements definitely gave an impression that the film was trying to gain wide appeal to various demographics, not just martial arts film fans but also fans of Blaxploitation and Bond films, so from time to time there would be a "Everything and the kitchen sink" feel when the film would suddenly focused itself on other characters played by John Saxon, Jim Kelly and Ahna Capri. I also felt that the film's middle scenes with Bruce Lee's character exploring Han's island at night could've been more action packed with additional fights between Lee and the guards, instead of holding them back until the finale.

I think had Lee written the film's screenplay himself like he did in "Way of the Dragon", the film would've been much more focused on his character instead of devoting time to the other characters with their backstories, and that Lee would probably be the only person going to the island and participating in the tournament.

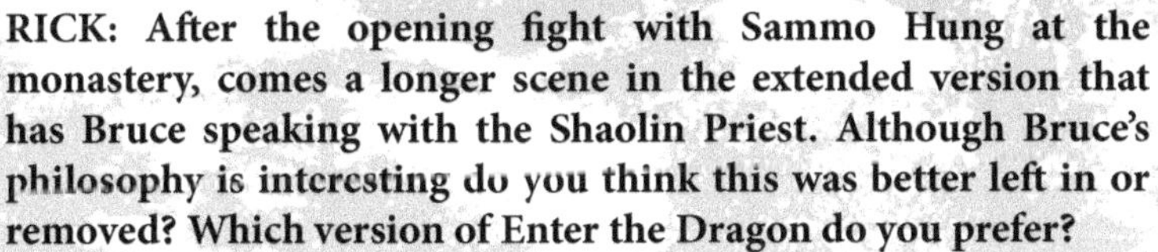

RICK: After the opening fight with Sammo Hung at the monastery, comes a longer scene in the extended version that has Bruce speaking with the Shaolin Priest. Although Bruce's philosophy is interesting do you think this was better left in or removed? Which version of Enter the Dragon do you prefer?

FRANK: I am probably the wrong person to ask this question since I am a completist when it comes to both film and music (Haha!). For example, I have almost all the recorded versions of Wagner's Ring cycle operas (In studio and live!). I want to watch everything that was shot for a film, either integrated into the film as an extended version like the scene between Bruce and Roy Chiao who played the priest, or included as deleted scene/ special feature on the disc. I've always felt an extended version of any film shows more of the director's intentions and the extra scenes were usually cut due to time constraints or studio interference, and so to me the longer the film, the better! So many times I've watched a deleted scene of a film and thought it should have been included.

And since I saw the extended version of "Enter the Dragon" first, I had always felt this scene belongs in the film organically and it would've been odd if I watch the film now with this scene removed. I feel the dialogue between Bruce and Roy (and also the later scene with Bruce and a very young Stephen Tung Wai) was crucial in conveying his character's mental maturity and wisdom and that he's more than just a rogue agent hired by British intelligence. It also gives the film a breather, to allow audiences to "slow down" so to

to this mysterious island to compete in a martial arts tournament hosted by this equally mysterious crime lord. Bruce was probably at his best physical shape while making this movie, and the final battle in the underground dungeon prison was fantastic (though with the exception of Shek Kin's Han in the final fight and Rob Wall's O'Hara whom he fought in the tournament, Lee's opponents were mostly faceless). It made an international star out of Angela Mao in her oh-so-brief appearance, and you had an iconic villain in Shek

speak so that Bruce can give us a valuable glimpse into his mindset as he reveals his personal beliefs and philosophy in martial arts. Going off the tangent for a moment though (Since you did ask which version of Enter the Dragon do I prefer), the true version that I prefer would be the one in which 1. Angela Mao didn't die and she went to the island with Bruce and they eventually fought Mr. Han TOGETHER. Imagine how amazing that would have been? 2. John Saxon didn't bite Bolo (that's playing dirty and should've never been included) and didn't kick Bolo in the nuts, Bolo defeats John Saxon and he ended up fighting Bruce mano a mano in the finale.

RICK: In hindsight do you think Enter the Dragon was Bruce Lee's defining role in terms of cementing his iconic status to the world, or did he have better roles in his other films and the only reason Enter the Dragon is the most cited is due to it being a Hollywood production?

FRANK: Many Bruce Lee fans would consider ENTER THE DRAGON to be his best film. It has a great plot with Bruce traveling

Kin's Han. And when it comes to production value, ENTER THE DRAGON really shines--after all, it was a Hong Kong/Hollywood co-production. I think that's the main reason why it's the most cited. I feel that ENTER THE DRAGON is certainly Lee's most ICONIC film but it has certain elements that prevented it from being his best, due to the several reasons I mentioned before.

If I have to choose one Bruce Lee film as his best, then it would certainly be THE WAY OF THE DRAGON. It was Lee's first directorial effort, it starred him as the lead, he wrote the script, he choreographed the action, and he co-produced it. Unlike ENTER with the various subplots among other characters, WAY focused solely on his Chan Lung character from this fish-out-of-water lad traveling from Hong Kong to Rome to help out his uncle, to finally becoming the "Dragon"--the hero of the film. The character and the story arc were much more interesting for me than his character in ENTER THE DRAGON who was rather one-note. The comedy in the beginning of WAY was also a nice touch that befits his new-kid-in-town characterization and I like how we saw a rare display

between her and Lee, they never got together in the end with Tong Lung walking away from her (and Rome) Cowboy-like into the sunset.

Then there's the classic fight with Chuck Norris, a masterpiece in fight strategy, choreography, and psychology between the two fighters in an actual contest. I love how Bruce's Tong Lung first gets a serious beating from Norris which led to him changing his fight tactics in order to defeat Norris, and how at the end of the fight there were all these wordless glances between them--the unspoken understanding between two warriors that Norris, samurai/gladiator-like, simply would not and could not admit defeat and would rather be killed by Lee than lose. I feel there isn't a fight in ENTER THE DRAGON that can be compared with this fight when it comes to showcasing Lee's incredible athleticism, skill, and philosophy as a martial artist here. The final fight between Lee and Shek Kin's Han in ENTER was great, but it's not on the same level (Incidentally, Warner Brothers originally wanted Lee to fight Han Ying-Chieh, the villain Lee fought in THE BIG BOSS, as the Hollywood studio wanted a rematch between them, which was why the villain's name in ENTER THE DRAGON was Han, but Lee insisted on having Shek Kin play Han so the rematch did not materialize).

To name Bruce Lee's best film is always going to be subjective--it's a matter of personal opinion, taste and preference. But for me personally I would go with WAY OF THE DRAGON as his best film.

A special thank you to Frank for taking part in this Q&A

of Bruce's playfulness that's supposedly a reflection of how he really was in real life, and how the comedy gradually goes away once the film's bad guys enter the picture. And Nora Miao was at her most charming here among her collaboration with Lee and I also love the fact that, while the film certainly showed a possible attraction

PHOTO
GALLERY

佛

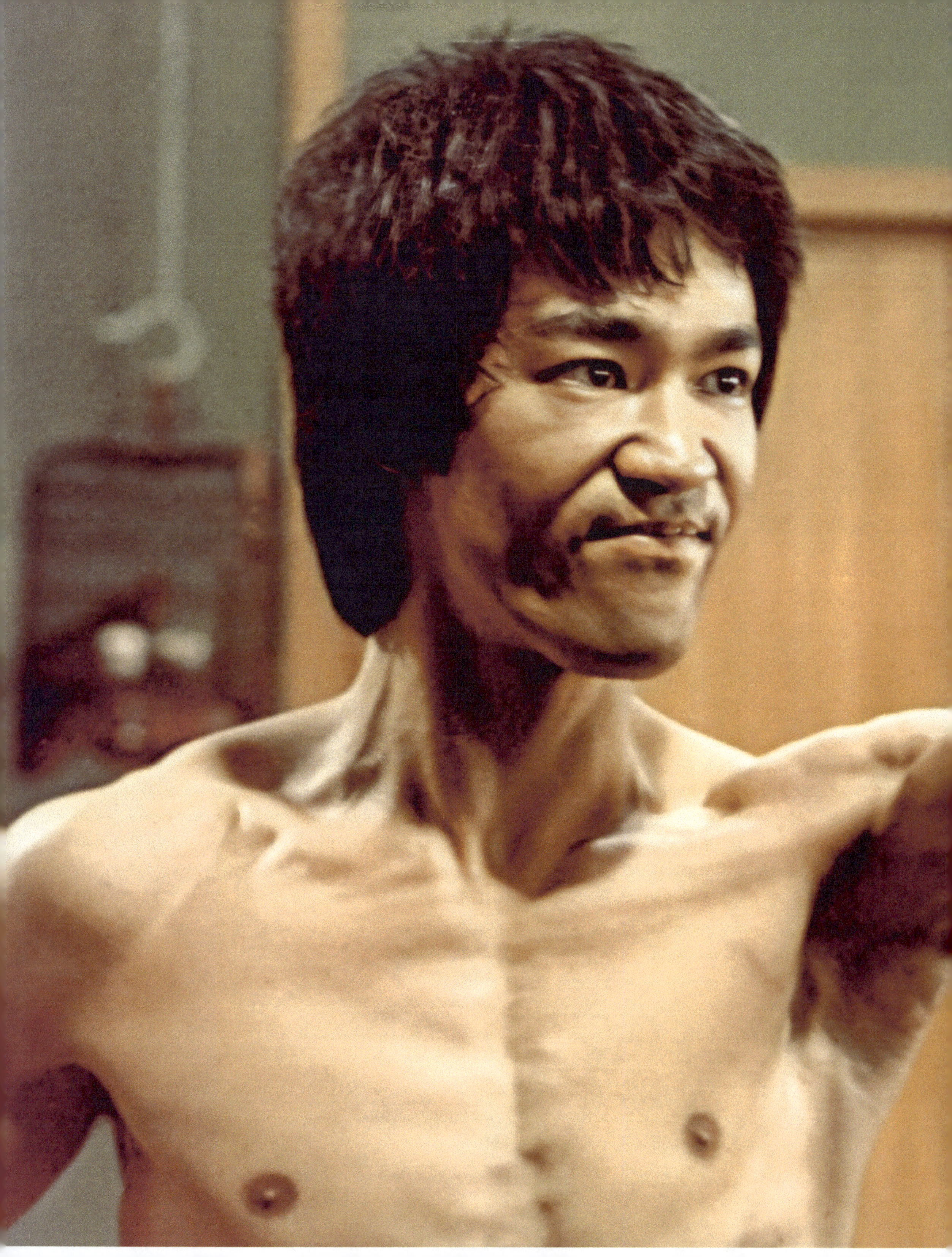

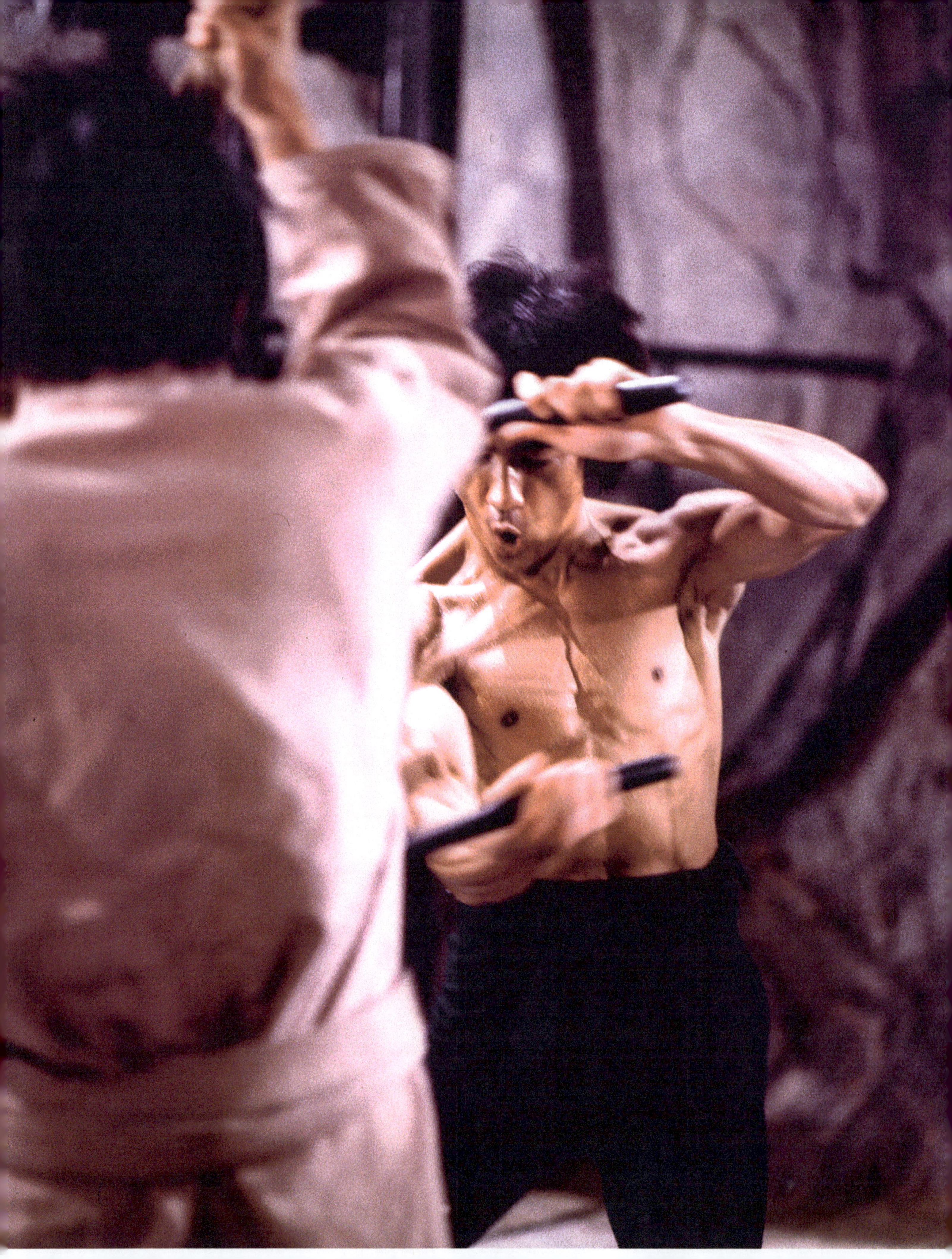

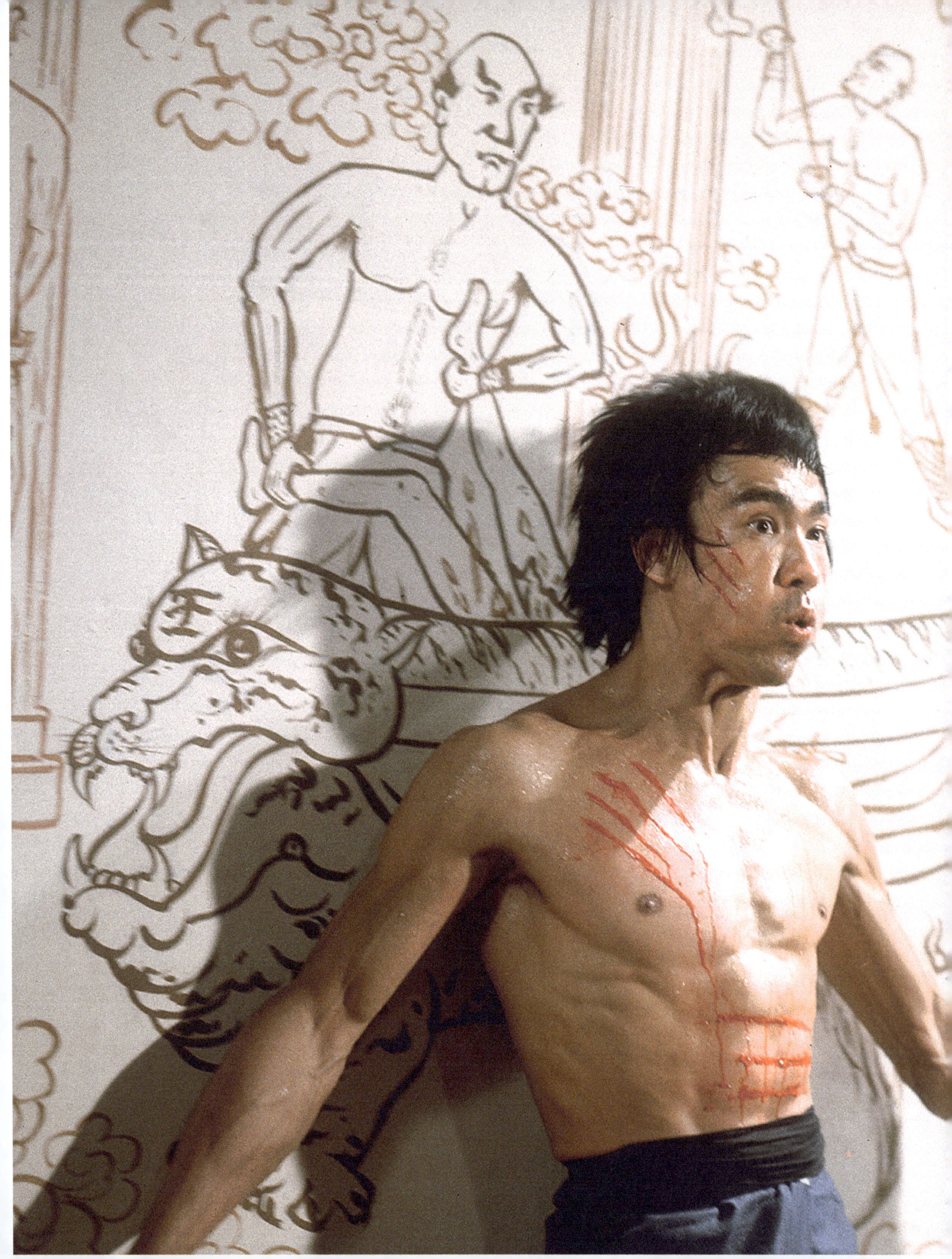

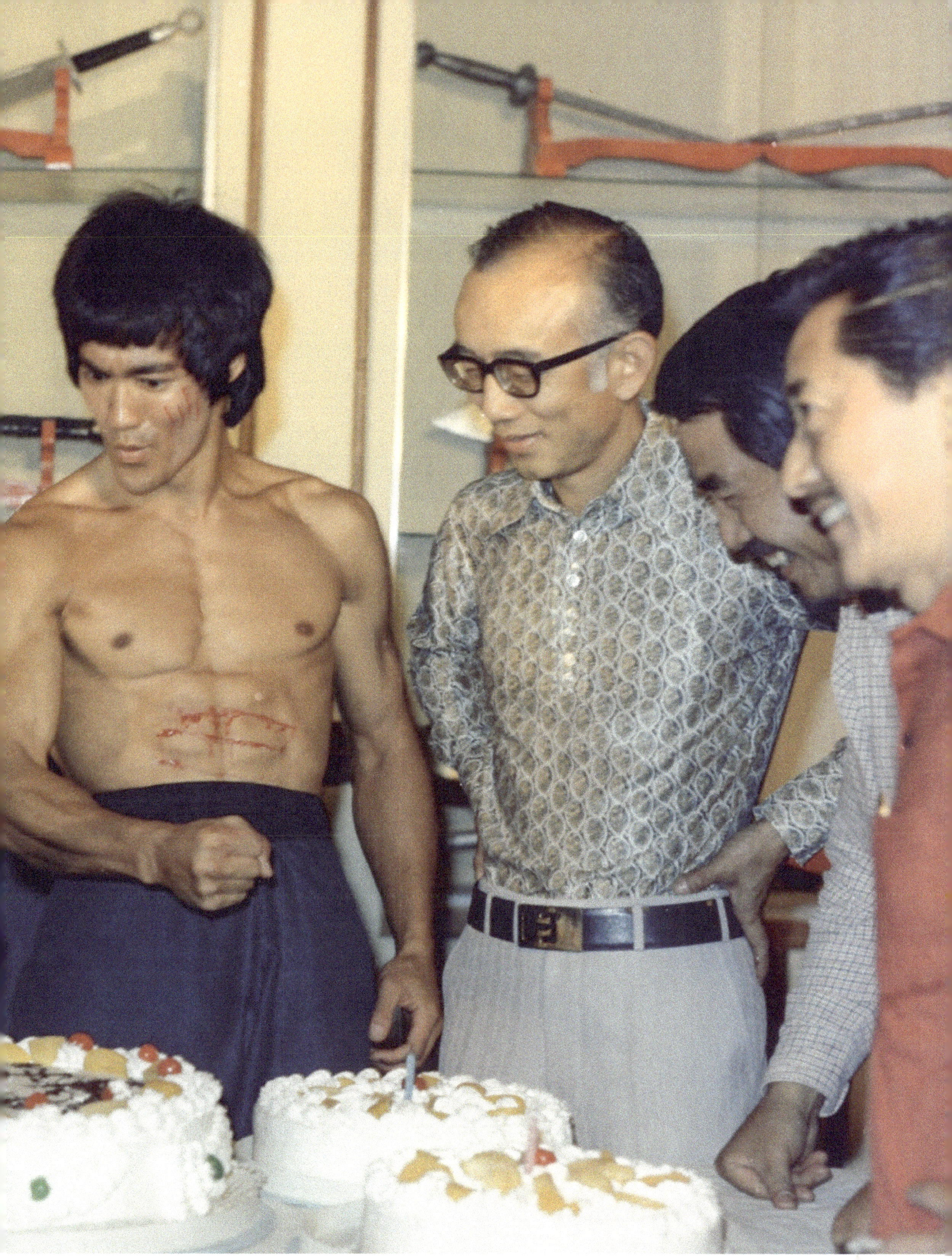

Enter The Dragon
Chapter 1

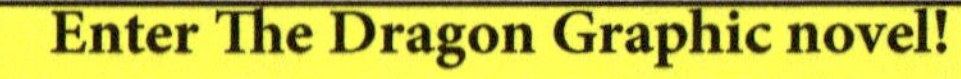

READY!
AND!
FIGHT!!

KUNG FU COMICS
Enter The Dragon
#1
2023
THE GREATEST
MARTIAL ARTS
MOVIE EVER...
..AND THE
ONLY
GRAPHIC
NOVEL TO
BRING IT
TO YOU.
ARTIST
MIKE KELLY
EDITOR
JOEL KELLY

BRUCE LEE

By Johnny Burnett

I'm sitting down to write this article on the 20th July, exactly 50 years to the day since Bruce Lee died, and it's this 50th Anniversary that has inspirednot only this wonderful special Eastern Heroes Enter The Dragon Issue which you're holding in your hands right now but also two brand new Physical Media releases of Bruce's work onto 4K UHD Disc and Bluray.

It's these two very special releases which I'll be diving into here, one absolutely packed, mammoth sized boxset from Arrow Video celebrating Bruce's HK movies and one new Warner Brothers release finally giving us a new 4K transfer of Enter The Dragon.

Bruce Lee at Golden Harvest
Arrow Video
4K UHD / Region B Bluray
UK Only Release.
Available Now.

I teased out this release last issue when we had just had the details of the boxset announced from Arrow, but the 17th July saw the set being officially released in the UK and what a truly incredible achievement it is. Absolutely THE most definitive release of Bruce Lee's work presented on Physical Media anywhere in the world, it's very, very hard to imagine this will ever be topped. As mentioned above, its official title is 'Bruce Lee at Golden Harvest' and the boxset is very definitely focused principally on Bruce's movies made at GH. The most impressive extras, restorations and extra footage all relate back to those four films, and whilst Enter The Dragon is included in the set, it's best to consider it a bonus extra rather than the main attraction here. As Warner's had long planned to release their own new 4K UHD edition of ETD, Arrow were only allowed to include the old 40th Anniversary Bluray as an extra on the set. So for anyone who already has that release, the transfer and extras are identical to that disc. We'll get to Warner's 4K release later on in the article, but let's dive properly into the wealth of new footage and incredible bonus features that Arrow have been able to put together for their flagship boxset.

It's worth noting first there are THREE different editions of the Arrow boxset available.All three sets contain 10 discs, but vary with the inclusion of 4K UHD discs for the 4 main Golden Harvest Films over regular Blurays in two of the sets… There are Two 'Red' Sets both with Artwork by the wonderful Tony Stella, these are identical in terms of on disc extras and artwork and differ only in one of them offering a mix of 4K UHD discs and Blurays and the other Red set being entirely on Bluray (and is a little cheaper as a result) the Third set or the 'Yellow' box version, is identical to the Red 4K boxset in content but differs in its cover art and individual artwork inside the box, on the yellow set this is all by Tom Ralston.

For my American friends please note that if you want to pickup any version of the boxset, all the Bluray discs are Region B locked, so will require a Multi Region player for you to be able to view the content…

All three boxes come with a 200-page hardbound book featuring new writing by Walter Chaw, Henry Blyth, Andrew Staton, Dylan Cheung, David West and James Flower, Twenty-four lobby card reproductions, 6 cards for the Big Boss, 6 for Fist of Fury, 6 for Way of the Dragon and 6 for Game of Death. Ten glossy photos of Lee in action printed on High Quality Photographic paper.
and a reversible poster with vintage quad poster artwork for The Big Boss and Way of The Dragon.

As for the discs themselves, let's take them individually there is an absolute mountain of content contained on them. I've been working through the Red 4K boxset, this will be identical to the Yellow box version, though obviously if you opt for the regular Bluray boxset, NO 4K discs will be present…

Disc One - The Big Boss - 4K Ultra HD Bluray

This is a brand new 4K (2160p) UHD Blu-ray presentation of the 99-minute 1983 version of The Big Boss, newly restored by Arrow Films from the original negative

And looks exceptional, the colours are far more vibrant and the restoration is first rate. The film looks absolutely magnificent!

We get newly restored lossless audio tracks of the original Mandarin, English and Cantonese dubs all in Mono with newly translated English subtitles.

Two brand new feature commentaries have been provided for the movie, one by David Desser and one by the insanely knowledgable Brandon Bentley AKA Old Pang Yao, who was instrumental in working behind the scenes as a producer on the boxset and cut together many of the supplementary extras as well as working on the audio files. I recently interviewed Brandon for my Youtube channel, and for anyone curious about the work he completed on the set, please do check out the conversation we had. Brandon has often spoken about the Big Boss being his all time favourite movie and his audio commentary track gives him a chance to share the wealth of information he has accumulated over the years about the movie and it's production. He's an excellent commentator, and this track is one of his very best. Absolutely first rate, I'm sure even the most die hard Bruce fans will find some new information here. Moving into the supplements we get 'Return to Thailand' a brand new documentary produced and presented by frequent Eastern Heroes contributor Matt Routledge exploring the original filming locations of the movie in Thailand.

This is also highly entertaining and extremely informative. Matt has put together a great documentary and will be taking the documentary out and screening it publicly in Birmingham in August at the Mockingbird Cinema along with Enter The Dragon and will be in attendance for a Q+A as well. if you can get down to Drum definitely worth checking it out on the big screen! We also get some newly uncovered deleted and extended scenes, with optional commentary by Brandon Bentley (more on these when we get to disc two!)

Brandon has also created a short documentary piece entitled 'The Not-Quite-Biggest Boss'. This is a video essay investigating the scenes still lost, and covers the much debated (and still lost to time) 'saw-in-the-head' scene.

We get some old Hong Kong Legends Archive interviews with co-star Lau Wing and stuntman Tung Wai taken from the old DVD release. Bruce Lee Vs. Peter Thomas is a new a short video essay about the music for the English version, short but fascinating. the disc is rounded out with Alternate credits sequences and a trailer gallery, including a 'Before The Big Boss' reel and the trailer for lost sequel The Big Boss Part II as is standard place for Arrow' boxsets we also get a hefty Image gallery.

All in all a wonderful disc, but for fans of the Big Boss, it's really disc two that will likely bring the most excitement….

Disc Two - The Big Boss - the Mandarin Cut (4K Ultra HD Bluray)

Here we get three alternate versions of The Big Boss all with lossless mono audio, and all newly restored by Arrow Films: Most notable to fans will be the rare (and longer) 110-min Mandarin Cut, This uses seamless branching to reinsert the scenes lost in the 1993 version of the film but you also get the option to watch the 100-min English Export Cut, featuring a rare alternate English dub track (some scenes in Mandarin); and the 100-min US Theatrical Cut

The new scenes are mostly slightly longer takes with James Tien's character, some more of Nora Miao (always a welcome sight) and most notably another visit by Bruce to the brothel. It's interesting to see these scenes back installed into the film, though you will notice a slight quality dip from the new 4K restoration to these elements when they come round.

As disc one got the bulk of the new supplemental materials for the movie, disc two only adds one more video essay titled 'Axis of English' This essay by Will Offutt profiles the English dubbing actors for The Big Boss, Fist of Fury and The Way of the Dragon and was a real treat, it must have been an incredible time to be working as a voice over artist back in HK in this period. It's always a treat to get a spotlight shone on the voices many of us know so well. Arrow have also provided a completely Unrestored raw scan of the Mandarin Cut which is great to show just how far we've come in terms of film restoration and will also scratch that nostalgic itch for those who remember seeing grainy, washed out VHS copies of the Big Boss back in the 80's!

Disc Three - Fist of Fury (4K Ultra HD Bluray)

Fist of Fury is for me, Bruce's best HK movie overall, when Arrow announced a series of cinema screenings to help promote the release of their boxset in UK cinemas, it was Fist of Fury we raced to book tickets for, seeing it on the big screen for the first time was an incredible experience. And really gave me a chance to see up close and personal just how wonderful a job Arrow have done with the new restorations. I already had Criterion's excellent Bruce Lee His Greatest Hits boxset on bluray (US only) so was unsure just how much the work on the Criterion set could have been improved upon. but Arrow really have done a remarkable job. Fist of Fury looks brighter, more vibrant and sounds absolutely incredible.

I was happy to see the 4K UHD disc faithfully reproduces this experience when watched at home but also adds the benefit of offering an Alternate 'English Export Cut viewing option' which lets you choose different opening and closing credits by using seamless branching.

The Mandarin, English and Cantonese mono audio tracks have all been restored and sound first rate, we actually get Two English mono options, the standard mix as well as a Japanese mix with alternate music (and slightly different cues, again please check out with interview with Brandon Bentley over on YouTube for more information on this aspect of the release)

Arrow have again provided two brand new feature commentaries for the movie, one by the wonderful Jonathan Clements and one by Brandon Bentley. Brandon has actually provided a new track for every one of the Golden Harvest movies on the boxset, and his track here is exceptional. I've also long been a big fan of the writer Jonathan Clements and his Audio Commentaries are the stuff of legend for Anime fans (who tend to call them Clementaries) Jonathan always brings a wonderful mix of humour and knowledge to his tracks, and his track for Fist of Fury is right up there for me with his other work for Arrow video on their Shawscope boxsets.

Another Arrow video veteran, the film critic and historian Tony Rayns presents 'Legend of the Dragon' an 80-minute overview of Lee's life and career which may delight or infuriate some fans depending on your perspective of Rayns, he's never shy of offering his own opinions and I've always found his insights highly entertaining even when i may not always share his point of view. This is a wonderful essay though.

Another brand new featurette entitled 'Visions of Fury' offers new interviews with co-producer Andre Morgan and martial arts expert (and Eastern Heroes contributors) Michael Worth and Frank Djeng. We also get interviews with the wonderful John Kreng, Andy Cheng and Bruce Willow.

Nice to see more Archive Hong Kong Legends interviews ported over too,
here we get interviews with co-stars Nora Miao, Riki Hashimoto, Jun Katsumura and Yuen Wah. The Fist of Fury disc is rounded out with an Alternate credits sequence
and a great Trailer gallery, including a wonderful Chen Zhen trailer reel and an Image gallery. This may well be the disc I revisit most often from the set. Absolutely first class.

Disc Four - The Way Of The Dragon (4K Ultra HD Bluray)

Again another beautiful new restoration by Arrow Films from the original film elements, here offering the Hong Kong Theatrical Cut and the Japanese Cut via seamless branching.

Way of the Dragon has always been a firm fan favourite and for some this disc will be the best of the boxet, the movie has been well served in terms extras and again Arrow has commissioned not one, but two brand new feature commentaries, one by the Master of Remaster himself Frank Djeng, joined here by the wonderful Michael Worth and a second solo track again by Old Pang Yao / Brandon Bentley Both tracks are excellent, with how much these movies have been discussed over the years, its hard to imagine finding out anything new from Audio commentaries for those of us who have been here since the old Hong Kong Legends days, but both tracks here are exceptional. Brandon's track finds him in his element again, never happier than when chatting about Bruce and his legacy and Frank and Michael bounce off each other very well. Fans of 88 films and Eureka's recent wave of HK movies on bluray will be familiar with them and they bring the magic to this track once more.

Michael offers a very cinematography and Martial Arts perspective to proceedings whilst Frank dives deep for more cultural and factual nuggets. Audio Gold on both commentaries here!

For Way of the Dragon extra features we get 'The Way of the Camera' A wonderful new documentary looking at Lee's filmmaking and fighting method in Way of The Dragon, featuring interviews with Golden Harvest producer Andre Morgan, Michael Worth, Jon Kreng, Andy Cheng, Frank Djeng, David Yeung, film historian Courtney Joyner and actors Piet (Peter) Schweer, Jon Benn and John Saxon - this was fascinating. Meet the Italian Beauty, a newly filmed interview with star Malisa Longo, this will definitely piss a few of the most devoted Bruce Lee fans off a little as it becomes quite clear that Malisa Longo isn't much of a fan of the movie, nor of Bruce himself.
She also has a weird recollection of the little dragon suggesting that his English wasn't great (which is a little weird she remembers it that way) It's a fun wee extra though.

We also get 'The Scottish Soldier Meets the Dragon' this was kinda cool for me as a fellow Scotsman, a newly filmed interview with on-set observer John Young. quite short, but very sweet. The last Newly produced piece for disc four is a select scene commentary by 'thug' actor Piet Schweer, this is cool, he offers interesting memories of his time on set. Back to the old HKL Archives again for interviews with co-stars Jon Benn, Bob Wall and Hwang In-shik and production managers Chaplin Chang and Louis Sit Can probably sell my old HKL DVD boxset now. think it's pretty much redundant now! We also get a Trailer gallery which includes a pretty excellent Bruceploitation trailer reel, just in time for Michael Worth and Frank Djeng's 'Enter The Clones of Bruce Lee' documentary being released onto the world! Oh, and almost forgot the Image gallery, which is cool, but the lobby cards that come bundled with the boxset are cooler. It's nice to have photos in hand.

Disc Five - Enter The Dragon (Region B Bluray)

As previously mentioned, this is included really as a bonus extra, it's a straight copy of the warner Brothers 40th Anniversary blu-ray release, with all the extras that were on that disc present here. It's still cool to have it included inside the boxset though, in a nice Digibook case with the international poster on the outside and the HK poster on the inside. Extras wise, it's just the same old Feature commentary by writer Michael Allin and producer Paul Heller that's been on every ETD release since the DVD and the No Way As Way and Wing Chun: The Art that Introduced Kung Fu to Bruce Lee, Return to Han's Island, Blood and Steel: The Making of 'Enter the Dragon', Bruce Lee: In His Own Words and Backyard Workout with Bruce featurettes as well as The Curse of the Dragon documentary and the old Interviews with Linda Lee Cadwell

Just consider it a bonus extra, if you're really, really jonesing for Enter the Dragon in 4K, as mentioned earlier, Warner's have their own release coming soon, but more about that later in the article.
It's in Bruce's last HK movie that the Arrow boxset really shines the brightest. A film much maligned in it's original cinematic release state back in 1978,

And essentially the first (and arguably most egregious) brucesploitation project of all time. But a film that even back then offered a tantalising glimpse of what could have been had Lee not passed away before being able to return to finish the project he started in 1972. We have seen several attempts at honouring Lee's original vision over the years, from Hong Kong Legends in the early noughts through to Alan Canvan's Game of Death redux project, but with this boxset, Arrow have really dived in deep and dedicated three discs to the film, it's enduring interest to fans and its powerful legacy.

Disc Six - Game of Death (4K Ultra HD Bluray)

The 4K disc offers both the international and Japanese cut of the movie, both lovingly restored and looking absolutely incredible.
The commentary track for the movie here is provided once again by Brandon Bentley though here he is joined by Big Mike Leeder. It's one of my favourite tracks on the set, Mike adores Game of Death, embraces all it's flaws and celebrates it for what it is. And he and Brandon do a great job of detailing the how's, why's and where's of it all. It's a fantastic listen, Bravo Gentlemen!
We get a newly filmed interview with star Colleen Camp who is a much more respectful and engaged interviewee than Malisa Longo.
We see the Deleted and extended scenes from the Chinese-language versions of the film, including two alternate endings The old HKL deluxe DVD edition has offered up some great Archive interviews which are a welcome addition here, with co-stars Dan Inosanto and Bob Wall.
The fascinating Behind-the-scenes footage as featured in Bruce Lee: The Legend are also on the main movie disc along with a Rare pre-production sales featurette from 1976 which Michael Worth and producer Andre Morgan have provided a new commentary for.
Arrow have also added Sammo Hung's fight scenes dailies (a small taste of what's to come on disc eight) A vintage Locations featurette from 2013 a Trailer gallery, including more Bruceploitation clips and a 'Robert Clouse at Golden Harvest' trailer reel and of course, an Image gallery.

Disc Seven - Game of Death Alternate Versions (Region B Bluray)

Disc seven offers up the Chinese versions of the movie with both Mandarin and Cantonese language options and uses seamless branching to offer two alternate versions with different credits, different ending and reinstating the Hapkido master Ji Han-Jae's fight. It also pulls more from the old HKL DVD set and offers up the Archive interview with Casanova Wong from 2001 and several key featurettes on Lee's life and impact: The Hong Kong Connection, Bruce Lee Remembered, Legacy of the Dragon, Dragon Rising and The Grandmaster & The Dragon, featuring interviews with Hung, Donnie Yen, William Cheung and many others.
More Archival interviews with Robert Lee, Phoebe Lee, Pat Johnson, George Lee, Gene LeBell, Van Williams, Joe Torrenueva, Jeff Imada, Linda Palmer, Fred Weintraub, Tom Kuhn, Paul Heller and James Lew round out the disc.

Disc Eight - Game of Death Bonus Disc (Region B Bluray)

This dear friends, is where the real big draw of the boxset for a great many people can be found. All eleven reels of footage that lee shot for Game of Death, every take, every scene, every clapperboard strike. Presented in its entirely with a fascinating voiceover by lead Arrow Producer James Flower. This 3.5 hour video essay makes for absolutely fascinating viewing. You can see a glimpse into Lee's working methods, his attention to detail, and how he would evolve and refine shots over multiple takes.
 Brandon Bentley and Arrow have also presented a new assembly of Lee's footage with new dubbing and new credit sequence more in keeping with Lee's other HK movies which you can find at the end of the main documentary.
 We also finally get to see the long thought lost 'Log Fight' sequence with Chieh Yuan facing off against Dan Inosanto as well as the short test clips Bruce shot in the New Territories with Hwang In-shik which gives a tantalising glimpse of what Bruce had in mind for the other levels of the Pagoda!.
 It's worth the cost of the boxset all on it's own, but is just the tip of the iceberg for what on offer here over the rest of the movies on the boxset. However, it is this video essay I think will make the most lasting impact and impression on fans. It's an absolute treat to behold and my heartfelt kudos to Arrow for having the good sense to put all eleven reels up on show, warts and all.
 Disc eight also contains the old Hong Kong Legends assembly, Game of Death: Revisited from 2001, Super 8 footage from 1974 of Dan Inosanto demonstrating the nunchaku a brief archival interview with Kareem Abdul-Jabbar from 1976 and you guessed it, an Image gallery.

Disc Nine - Game of Death II / Tower of Death (Region B Bluray)

Making it's UK Bluray debut we also get the other key Bruceploitation movie to actually contain footage of the man himself in it, Game of Death II / Tower of Death. Here presented in a new 2K restoration again by Arrow themselves (and again looking magnificent) We get the international cut (Game of Death II)
as well as the Hong Kong Cut (Tower of Death) Tower of Death is just a 1080p presentation but still looks fantastic.
Frank Djeng & Michael Worth return for commentary duties and

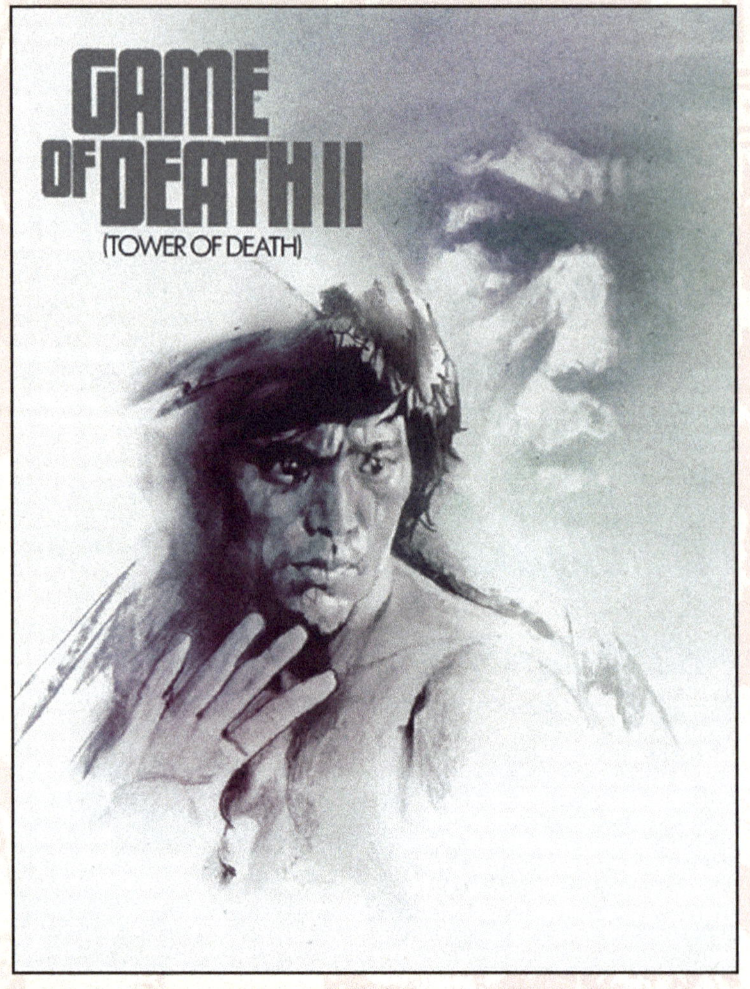

to help make sense of the various different versions of the movie.
 Arrow have also added the Alternate Korean version with it's unique footage, again presented in High Definition as well as an alternate US video version again presented via seamless branching. It's a film with much to find interesting.
 And also acts as a taste of what's to come in Severin Films upcoming Brucesplitation boxset(s). There is also the alternate end credits sequence for Game of Death II and of course, Trailer and image galleries.

Disc Ten - Documentaries (Region B Bluray)

Arrow have also taken the time to properly remaster the two best known Bruce Lee Documentaries, Bruce Lee the Man & The Legend (1973) and Bruce lee the Legend (1984). We get the original Mandarin Audio for The Man and the Legend and English tracks for both films and new subtitles for both.
 There is also a fascinating Archive video tour of Golden Harvest Studios conducted in the mid-1990s by Russell Cawthorne, writer of Bruce Lee: The Legend as well as Alternate animated Hong Kong credits for Enter the Dragon and Trailers and image gallery for both films and that's pretty much the full line-up - it's likely going to be a shoe in (or flying kick in) for physical media release of the year by a long shot. And it's very, very hard to imagine how anyone will be able to one up what Arrow have put together here.
 If you're on social media at all, you'll likely have seen a degree of frustration from buyers of the boxset receiving their boxes with dents due to somewhat lacklustre packaging from the warehouse handling the orders for Arrow, but don't let that sway   your decision to pickup the set, nor dwell on the out box

too much, or you'll miss all the heavenly glory contained within!! It's an absolute labour of love, respect and admiration from the producers at Arrow and from their key contributors and collaborators. It's an absolute triumph of a release and one I emplore you all to track down, if you don't want to, or can't afford to spend the cash on the boxset, then you can check out all the contents on Arrow Video's online player. Available via their own app, or via Amazon Prime Streaming.

But however you watch it, just make sure you do! There are hours and hours of fascinating new bonus content, and THE best restorations of Bruce's Hong Kong Movies produced to date. Absolutely essential. 10/10.

Enter The Dragon Warner Brothers 4K/Bluray Steelbook Worldwide release. Available 11th September 2023

Arriving with a very lacklustre whimper in comparison to Arrow's incredible hard work, comes Warner Brother's own 'tribute' to the little dragon, their forthcoming 50th Anniversary release of Enter The Dragon due in early September. This is a bit of a letdown in terms of Warner's having produced zero new extras or content for the release that wasn't on the 40th Anniversary bluray ten years ago. The only big draw here is a hew 4K transfer and UHD disc release of the international cut and the shorter theatrical cut of the movie (which was previously available in standard Bluray on the Criterion boxset)

Time will tell how good the new Warner's 4K transfer looks but all the other on disc extras are identical to the 40th Anniversary release. It does feel like a bit of a wasted opportunity, but sadly Warner Brother's have a tendency to do this when it comes to the HK movies that they have in their catalogue

Don't get me started on their upcoming release of Rumble in the Bronx. That's a tale for another issue.

If you want to dive deeper into the Bruce Lee boxset, please check out my video interviews with Brandon Bentley, Big Mike Leeder and with Frank Djeng. You can find them all over on my youtube channel alongside unboxings, more reviews and news updates about upcoming releases..

www.youtube.com/thefanaticaldragon

BRUCE LEE
THE BIG BOSS

BRUCE LEE
THE WAY OF THE DRAGON

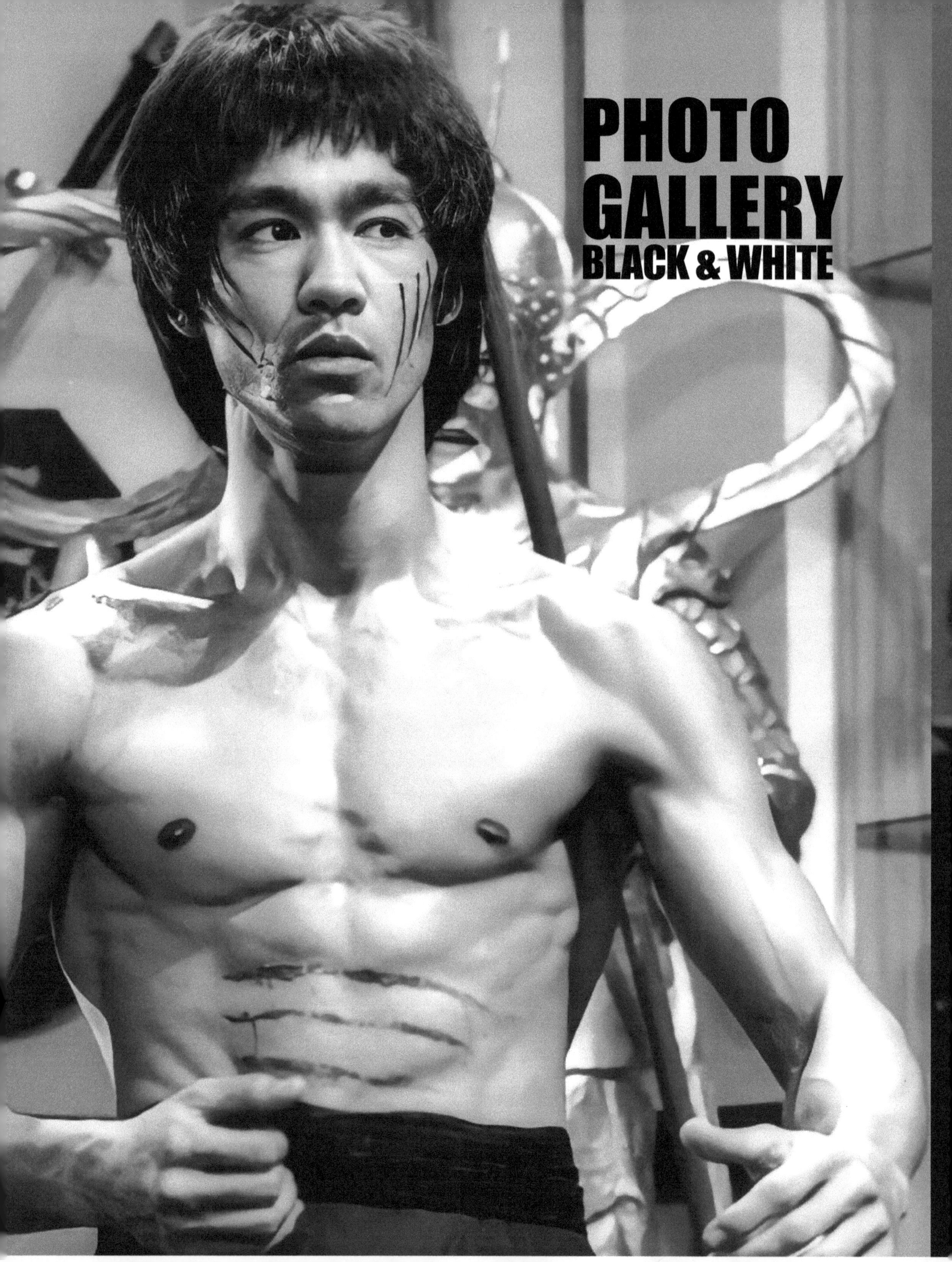
PHOTO
GALLERY
BLACK & WHITE

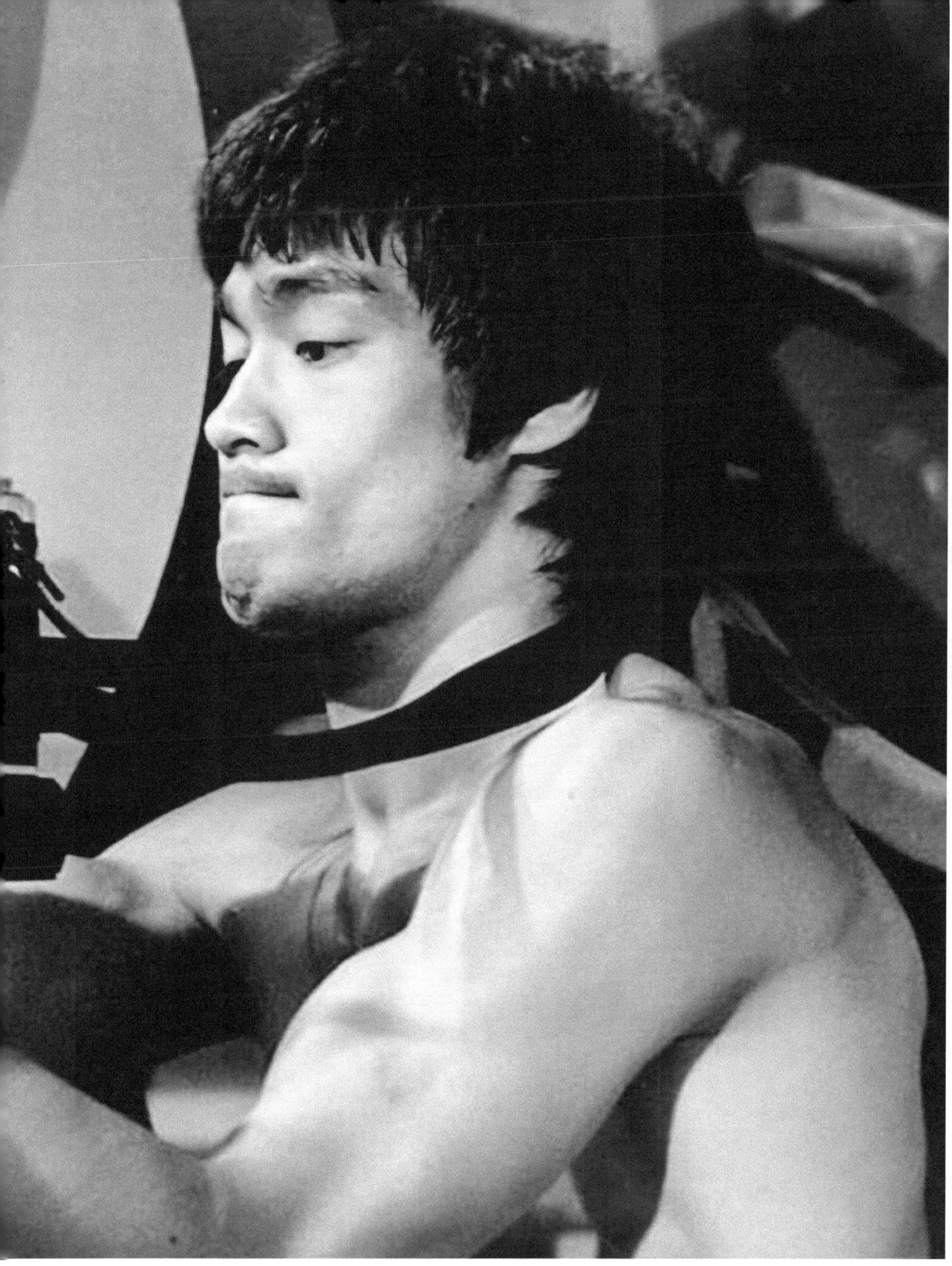

SPECIAL THANKS

Cover & Interior Design & Layout Tim Hollingsworth

Alan Canvan

Mathew Polly

Frank Djeng

Mike Kelly

Whom, without their valuable contributions,
this book could not have happened.